MW00885082

Donald J Berk

In Search of
WINGS
LOST

White Quill LLC

First Edition.
First Printing: August 2009

White Quill LLC

Yakima, Washington

ISBN: 1-4392-5721-3
ISBN-13: 9781439257210
Library of Congress Control Number: 2009909144

In memory of Janet Ellen Berk

*All literature waivers between nature and paradise
and loves to mistake one for the other.*

– Elias Canetti

Acknowledgements

My deep gratitude to the readers and writers and teachers who kept me going on this book when I wanted to quit.

Special thanks to Rachel Tecza, Debbie Brod, Laura Pepin, Brian Davis, Ann Brack, Joan O'Leary, Susan Anderson, Louise Parms, Jane Silberstein and Catherine Knepper for their invaluable suggestions and encouragement.

And to Elizabeth Cox, Askold Melnyczuk and Sven Birkerts for their patience with a plodder.

Finally, to Lily Reid for her superb illustrations.

I am also indebted to The Bloedel Reserve, Bainbridge Island, Washington, for permission to use its name and to the Bloedel docent whose spirited anecdote about a reclusive trumpeter swan inspired the story.

Chapter 1

I was hatched and raised on The Bloedel Reserve, Bainbridge Island, Washington. We had a nice climate there — maritime, a bit raw and shivery in winter, a rare dash of wet snow, only not so frozen one absolutely had to migrate. Father discouraged romantic notions of a nomadic life. "You have no idea what an ordeal it is for a flock to pull up drakes, Marcel," he'd say with the authority of experience. Years ago, he'd flown the half-day from his birthplace on Vancouver Island to Bloedel. After an overnight stopover, he'd decided to settle in rather than press on south with the rest of the flock.

Winter made me look forward all the more to spring — marvelous weeks of low, ragged clouds scudding by, dragging torrents of rain across the marsh, drenching the meadows, the wind tangy with the scent of mountain pine and ocean-chilled salt, sleepy bees plundering the trillium.

In any weather, Bloedel never lacked bustle. The air rang with vociferations—crow caws, owl screeches, hawk cries, robin warbles, goose barks, seagull pipes—all gossiping, Father would say, about every subject, without regard for the decency of truth. "A mallard ought to be spare with words, son—a drake deliberates, checks his data, makes his point and shuts up," he would lecture whenever I rambled on about something. "Just a grunt or two, Marcel. It's the highest level of discourse."

He would elaborate at length and with great eloquence on this topic, while I floated with my siblings on the marsh lake, giving him my attention, absorbing as much of his wisdom as is possible at that age and promising to work on my "habitual and polysyllabic aversion to brevity," as Father put it.

Meaning no disrespect to Father, Phoenix rest his soul, I did happen to believe that the evening song of the trumpeter swans transcended any other form of communication, harmony so vibrant that upon the first notes all gabble on the reserve halted—excepting the frogs and insects, who, owing to their coarser instincts, as Father would point out, particularly when he had a headache, could never restrain their throats and unruly body parts from servicing the calls of baser functions.

Right out of the egg, I was an ordinary duckling. That can be an advantage in a flock. You get to watch and learn and screw up with no one counting on your example.

"Marcel's going to be a plodder," Father observed, shaking his head with disappointment at my first attempts to clamber up a slick bank, my feet churning and backsliding in the mud.

"On land, Basil, we are all plodders," Mother counseled on my behalf—then, to me, "Flap a bit, dear, it helps."

It was quite sufficient for me to be ordinary, to blend in with my brothers and sisters—Troy, Keith and Harold (the double-yolkers), Phoebe and Basil Junior. Poor Basil Junior turned out to be female—it's not so easy to tell in the first week or two—and that caused some embarrassment, especially to Father, but one night an otter got him—her, that is—and then, sadly, the confusion became moot. Thereafter, Father would never refer to her by name—it was always, "the kid." I would like to say I was fond of Junior, but at that age we were simply clumsy amber feather balls, oblivious to all save our imprint of Mother—how to keep her in sight—and our insatiable quest for food.

The otters were cunning, and they were hungriest in the morning, especially before a storm. Father would eye the horizon and declare, "Red sky in the morning, mallard's warning." I took heed of this, and when I was older and more independent, generally enjoyed a late brunch rather than breakfast, allowing time for the otters to fill up on fish and frogs—took heed unfailingly, in fact, after my sister Phoebe was savaged right before my eyes.

The morning of our first birthday, she was floating a few yards offshore, digesting some aquatic roots, radiating feminine allure for the benefit of cruising young drakes. The water was dead calm, reflecting a red-orange dawn sky. Suddenly I spied a wake. A snub snout knifed the surface straight toward my sister. "Fly, Phoebe, fly!" I squawked as loud as I could. She glanced at me and spread her wings but it was too late. She went under, thrashing like a trout. We could smell her blood in the water for days. That evening, Edward Wingstrong, our reigning king and a most gifted trumpeter—simply an artist—played a requiem so sad I thought my heart would burst. Mother was inconsolable and Father wept openly. Unlike theirs, my grief was made impure by shame—how I had failed to rush to Phoebe's rescue.

"Don't punish yourself, Marcel," my brother Harold said. "What could you have done against an otter?" But shame is an infection that would worm into my heart.

The following morning, Father assembled a memorial procession of twenty ducks to paddle to the site of Phoebe's demise.

"What about the otters?" Mother asked.

"What about them?" Father said.

"Why, you'd all be sitting ducks out there."

"Damn the otters!"

But, as usual, Mother's wisdom prevailed and a flyby was decided upon instead of a flotilla. Ceremony seems a lame response to death by predator, a weak answer to any death, for that matter, but even if we had had the power to retaliate, I'm sure Phoebe would have wanted to be remembered rather than avenged—above all, birds want to be remembered.

And if we somehow could have had revenge, ducks can't eat otter, and only the buzzards and maggots would have been rewarded — as they are eventually, in any case.

After the memorial, Father's lesson to us was, "Remember this, children: always have someone to watch your back." At his glance I shrank into myself.

Generally, we webfeet don't like to be alone, and we seldom are. But there are always mavericks. Each of us was created differently, ornithologically speaking, so no matter how much you fret and worry you can't control someone else's behavior. Phoebe was a bit flighty, Phoenix rest her soul, and I'm certain that she drifted off by herself quite forgetful of the risk. My brother, Harold, fully conscious of the danger, would nevertheless spend an afternoon by himself inspecting the north bank for slugs. He wasn't the least bit scatterbrained, just independent.

For the unwary, other snares awaited. A month later, my cousin Irene was killed—a window crash, in this case. Rothbert Clout, the gamekeeper, had left a bowl of eggs on the table in his cabin. Irene's mind must have wandered—she had a profound nursing instinct—adding more grief to our mourning.

Despite the perils, there is no thrill like flight, and no point being a bird if you can't fly. Mother said that Pekin ducks, kiwis and ostriches can't fly any better than jackrabbits, but Father declared he could only assume it was a malicious rumor.

There are, of course, different flying styles. The raptors are magnificent, world-class aviators. I sometimes watched the golden eagles with awe — and, frankly, with blunt envy — as they soared on stiffened wings along the ridge, then suddenly tucked, hurtling down on their prey like feathered lightning. The hawks seemed to fly effortlessly, as well, just a little twitch here and there for course correction. Mind you, there are trade-offs in life—raw rodent makes a disgusting diet, not to mention what the vultures will settle for. As for the hummingbird, Father said the way their wings blur, the Almighty must have assembled them out of bumblebee parts.

We ducks, on the other wing, have to work hard in the air. We are endomorphs, and the same fat that keeps us warm in winter weighs us down aloft. It's flap, flap, flap, all the time.

Learning to fly broke you into the miracle of the third dimension—altitude. You felt as if you had conquered space and time, that you were omniscient, the sensation of weightlessness making you feel not only liberated from gravity, but suspended eternally in the present moment—an illusion, of course, since no matter how commanding your view, the future continued to rush at you from an invisible direction, often with stunning surprises.

From on high, the whole layout of the reserve was revealed—the black asphalt parking lot by the mansion, shimmering with summer heat, bright little cars strewn upon it like the jellybeans children threw at us; the wooden statue of Chief Wachu, who guarded the reserve's main gate, his tomahawk raised high, looking as if he had just finished carving himself from a tree trunk, and whom my brother Harold liked to dive bomb after a heavy meal; the visitors' trail snaking through the woods; and the Japanese garden with its clean, combed gravel, which Harold would also make a target. The gamekeeper's cabin, where Clout took refuge from the rain—humans not being waterproof—was just a tiny green box, and Clout a tiny grub in the box. And you could safely track the menacing shapes of the otters as they cruised the marsh waters.

Unfortunately, although altitude distanced you from much unpleasantness and difficulty, sooner or later hunger, thirst, fatigue—and the regular cycles when you lost your feathers molting—forced you down to occupy a specific place on Earth.

The specific places varied considerably as to comfort. Much of the reserve was thickly wooded and not suitable for webbed feet, but a prime acre of piquant green lawn bordering the road to the mansion on one side and the marsh on the other appeared from aloft to be dotted with scores of small white berries standing on their stems. These were the tundra swans, which had occupied it for a decade. According to Mother, they'd seized it from the mute swans. The mutes, fewer in number, fought hard but were driven out. They re-settled farther north on a field of inferior, chewier turf.

The mutes never ceased to plot their repatriation, hissing with rancor wherever they went. Their numbers grew steadily as each season a squadron of cousins glided in from the east. It was an unspoken fear on the reserve that without intervention war was inevitable.

Occasionally, I would make a short trip off the reserve with my brother, Harold. To the west lay Puget Sound, where you could watch a pod of humpbacked whales play. More daring than I, Harold once ventured east over the Cascade Mountains to view the great vine of the Columbia River winding through the desert, green orchards clinging to it, he reported, like parrot plumage.

Once you got to pumping your wings, you forgot about the effort. The pure grip of flight took over your very being. You felt yourself in a mystical zone between heaven and earth, free of all care. What a feast! The wind pressing against your breast feathers, the easy "sproing!" of shoulder tendons working, the heady fragrances of the sea, damp pines and mountain snow. There were also the unsavory smells of human presence, such as engine fumes and landfill, but these were easily avoided or ignored. Yes, the gift of wings was precious—too easily taken for granted.

Chapter 2

Normal hazards of life aside, my generation was fortunate to grow up in a period of relative peace, firmly governed by the trumpeter swans—by two generations of the Wingstrong family, to be exact. Our first trumpeter, Edward Wingstrong, a diplomat and warrior, had been delivered to the reserve, as Mother recounted, seven years before I hatched. Over time, Edward worked to forge a truce among our various militant factions and flocks—the jays, blackbirds, crows, hawks, chickadees and sapsuckers—and kept the tundra and mute swans in check. He brought calm where feuds had wracked Bloedel for years.

According to Mother, when the trumpeters arrived, she and Father were divided about putting outsiders in charge—royal swans or not. She'd considered it an honor, a feather in our caps, she said. But Father would shrug his wings. "What they got to be so hoity-toity about? They poop on the grass just like us." To Mother's annoyance, he'd parody the graceful, swaying gait of a swan, squawking in an exaggerated waddle. Later, as peace spread on the reserve, he would recant. He became a great friend and admirer of Edward.

Mother said Edward arrived one blustery March afternoon in a cage in the bed of Clout's green pickup truck. "Clout took him immediately to have his wings pinioned," she recalled, twisting her own wings at a grotesque angle in illustration, making me shudder.

Then Clout brought in Veronica, for a mate. Edward and Veronica would cruise the marsh lake, making friends, gaining respect, creating a dominion. They built a nest and soon afterward Veronica hatched three cygnets. "They were a majestic family, the five of them," Mother sighed. "At twilight, with the sky to the west a beautiful pink and gray, like a gutted salmon, Edward would send out a long, rich trumpet, so pure it would make you shiver down to your gizzard. Veronica would answer with a sweet blare that never failed to draw a tear from your father's eye."

"It was just before your brood hatched, Marcel," Father added. "You were a bit anticlimactic, frankly."

Edward and Veronica, with their young—Louis, the heir apparent, E. Minor, second-in-line, and daughter, the serene and stoic Melody, would sail each dawn to the west side of the island for breakfast. The otters were known to hang out on the east side—the Otterman Empire, as it was known. The cygnets, with their crimson bills and gray down, looked as vulnerable as any little goslings you ever saw. Their parents, of course, guarded them with keen vigilance. Edward propelled himself in the lead like one of those frigates coming out of Puget Sound, his head pivoting from port to starboard like a radar dish. Veronica followed aft, equally alert for trouble. If they felt handicapped by their crippled wings, you would never have guessed.

Edward, his wings pinioned, couldn't fly, but he wasn't as defenseless as my poor sister, Phoebe. His bill could chop like Chief Wachu's tomahawk. The otters knew it and gave Edward a wide berth. Still, the cygnets were tempting. From a safe distance, one of the otters, this one a sneak among thieves, began to reconnoiter the Wingstrongs' feeding area. He would make a few probes, his nasty snout tracing wide circles, but he would retreat in a hurry when Edward advanced on him. Edward was brave. He kept the otter at bay for many months, until the cygnets had matured—when, with their hormones kicking in, they exchanged their gray fluff for the shining white plumage of a swan.

You would have thought that the first thing an adolescent swan would want to do would be to fly the coop, as chickens say. Yet Louis and his siblings simply paddled along behind their parents, as always. Father shook his head when I mentioned this. "Don't know how to fly, do they?" he clucked dryly, with an I-told-you-so nod at Mother. "Parents can't teach 'em, what with their bloody wings pinioned like they are now, eh?"

It was true. As soon as we were ready, Father had trained me and my brothers and sisters to fly. "You are fledglings," he said. "It is time."

It was hard work, but Father urged us on, nipping at our tail feathers when we felt too lazy or distracted to launch off the pond. You thought you couldn't possibly do it. Then, one day, you flew.

Mother had sympathy and hope for the Wingstrong brood but Father was pessimistic. "Overprotected," he observed, as the young swans paddled by in obedient train behind their parents. "Edward had his taste of the sky before Clout got to him, but the young'uns, the males, anyway, will lack mettle when the chirps are down, when thrush comes to dove."

Still, all was honky-dory, as my uncle Blake used to say, until in late autumn a devastating influenza swept the reserve. The crows and starlings seemed particularly susceptible and a shocking number died. We ducks were largely spared, but at night hoarse quacks and gasps fractured the normal tranquility of our cove. For three months, fear and suspicion lurked in every eye. Families kept to themselves. Just when the worst seemed over, Edward caught the disease and in two days he was gone. "His lungs just filled up," Veronica sobbed. The following morning, she perished, too—victim of mortal grief, of love marooned, Mother said, lapsing romantic as she often would, despite her pragmatism, although Father noted that Veronica had been wheezing hard.

The reserve fell into stunned silence that day—excepting the frogs and insects, not a chirp or whistle. Nest maintenance went on hold. All training was suspended, the only activity not curtailed being feeding of the young, and then only the altricials, the precocials having to fast along with their parents.

The buzzards arranged a wake for Edward and Veronica, a vast, stately and somber event, lasting three full days and nights, the winter weather cooperating with a peppery snow—chilling, but blessedly preservative.

Tributes poured in, emissaries arrived from as far away as Portland and Boise, procession after parade of birds passing in review, in flight and afloat. The marsh was jammed chick to fowl and the low wailing of the mourners would rise and fall day and night like the tide. A choir flew in from Tacoma, featuring a solo dirge sung by a blue heron in what I thought a valiant alto, but admittedly in a somewhat prehistoric, croaky timbre, "a thoughtless if not disgraceful choice," Father opined, "for a requiem for trumpeter swans, and a bit of a diva, if you ask me."

Just behind us, another heron's voice said, "She's not so bad."

"With all due respect, sir," Father shot back, swiveling his head around half a turn, "I've heard better from a gull gagging on a fish." Father wasn't good with sorrow. It made him aggressive.

"I can see you are loyal to the deceased," the heron said. It was a green heron. I had never seen one before.

Father floated in silence for a moment, his bill quivering slightly, then turned back to face the choir.

Intrigued by the green heron, I asked if he nested at Bloedel.

"Sorghum," he said. "Northwest of here—Olympic Mountains, very remote."

"That's where the great Phoenix is supposed to live," I said, my bill opening in wonder.

"So they say," he croaked, looking away. He had a vibrant voice that seemed to resonate in the water so that you felt it come up through your body. "Come see for yourself."

I turned to ask Father if he had passed over Sorghum en route from Vancouver Island, and if we might go, but could see he was absorbed in the concert, now that the performing heron had stepped back into the chorus.

When I looked back, the stranger was gone.

In homage, even the tundras and mutes put aside their differences, together constructing a raft to bear the deceased, adorning it with white flowers—"like a delicate white ship on an eternal voyage," was how Aunt Olive described it, recalling with some dismay the perfunctory disposal of the charred remains of Uncle Blake, who last year flew into the high tension lines north of the reserve.

An honor guard of swans flanked the raft all the way to the final resting ground, downwind of our populated area and out of sight, where the buzzards could indulge without offending the rest of us.

It was vital to have an early succession of rule, since within a week of Edward's funeral, scuffles between the tundras and mutes had already broken out.

The double-crested cormorants were summoned to arrange a coronation for young Louis Wingstrong, heir-in-waiting, and last eligible trumpeter swan on the reserve. Louis was yet a bit young to take on such responsibility—"pipsqueak" was the term Father used—but I had faith in him and was full of admiration, especially for the power of his mind. Bobbing on the marsh lake at twilight, ever watchful for otters, we had had long conversations on the nature of the cosmos—or rather, to be less presumptuous, I had harked to Louis' profound insights, hoping to absorb even fragments of his understanding, and so as not to distract his train of thought, I seldom interrupted with a question.

"Cultivate the memory, Marcel," Louis would tell me. "Remember each exquisite feeling and sensation so that you can recall it at will. This is the mark of a disciplined mind, able to retain the past in total as if it were the present. The universe is simply the single perfect memory of itself from beginning to end — its own perfect story."

"Rubbish," Mother disagreed after I had related this to her and Father. "If I could recall a thing perfectly, I'd never be bothered to go to the trouble of trying to do it again. Why, I'd simply have to remember whatever it felt like the first time."

"Procreation, for example, son," Father put forth. "If you'll excuse my directness."

"Basil," Mother said, glancing at me.

"Well, it's a bloody good example, Doris," Father said, "and Marcel will be courting soon, if I'm not mistaken."

"Marcel is already mated, Basil."

"He is?"

Mother and Father made good points, but as much as I loved and respected my parents, they weren't deep thinkers like Louis.

"Of course, your father never has had a strong memory," Mother went on, shifting on the eggs, her eighth brood. "He has to refresh it quite often."

"Then praise Phoenix for short memories!" Father guffawed, while Mother looked away demurely. Then, turning somber, Father added, "But some things are best forgotten, truth be told."

A lump came to my throat.

"Now, Basil, no amount of brooding will bring back Phoebe or the others, bless their souls," Mother consoled, rolling her eyes to the evening sky, where some stars were beginning to blink on.

I'd noticed, actually, that my mind didn't remember everything equally. The best memories seemed to lack a lot of detail—just a collage of images and sounds washed over with happy feelings. Take, for example, my wedding with Madeline, may Phoenix rest her soul. The day we were mated comes back as a blissful jumble of flashbacks. Even our first ecstatic display is just a blur. Possibly the fermented apples—fermies—that her parents had catered had something to do with that. Nevertheless there is nothing specific, only an overall feeling of rhapsody that stirs in me when I recall that day we danced the toucan tango.

Still, I do remember how, right in the middle of the vows, my brother Harold caused a disruption with a clearly underage gosling, which is why he was no longer allowed to view ecstatic displays, and was urged by her parents to consider migration.

The bad memories, on the other wing, are riddled with particulars—Madeline's murder, later on, for instance. And when my sister Phoebe was killed I remember exactly the otter's angle of attack, how it sliced in out of the low, blinding sun, black water curling over its snout; its whiskers and eyes, its tiny white teeth, how Phoebe screamed her death-squawk, a sound that I felt in my bowels, in all honesty that caused me to lose control of them, not that ducks are particularly concerned about control in that regard, especially when in the water, but nevertheless proving how otter fear can render you helpless. Maybe the mind engraves these fine details of bad situations to keep us from getting in the same situation the next time.

Looking back, Louis's coronation was subdued and unremarkable, following as it did right upon the hind toes of the royal funeral. Father, Mother, Madeline and I watched as Louis, having just lost his parents, and clearly still in a state of shock, was ushered through the ceremony by a pair of solemn owls.

"Doesn't look much of a commanding figure, does he, Marcel," Madeline whispered to me. "Let's hope he rises to the occasion."

"He won't be rising any too high," Father retorted, overhearing. "E. Minor had his father's bearing, not Louis. A sad day for the reserve, truth be known."

E. Minor, Louis' brother, had already been shipped off the reserve by Clout, and his sister Melody, as a female, was ineligible for high office. But the exact timing of the clearest destiny can never be foreseen. Louis had enjoyed a carefree adolescence, and, to be frank, had been becoming more and more amorously distracted, to the detriment of his succession training. He would hurry every morning across the broad lawn leading to the great columned mansion, where, with the front door propped open in summer, he would park himself before the steps of the veranda to view the giant, gilt-framed swan portrait hanging on the wall of the vestibule.

Louis had become mesmerized by this painting. Rooted in the lawn, he would stare for hours. "I call her 'Odetta,'" he told me. "It seems the perfect name for a perfect swan."

"Smut!" Father scoffed upon seeing Louis planted in front of the great house. "It's offensive, I say—such suggestive pictures, displayed in public for the young to ogle!"

"And what were you doing at the mansion, Basil?" Mother inquired dryly, her tail twitching.

Father, averting his eye and reaching his bill to smooth a displaced back feather, replied, "Piano recital, dear."

Louis was captivated. It was apparent to us that he was ready for a mate, obvious even to Clout—to give a human more credit than generally deserved, Father said—who, as gamekeeper, solved the problem by bringing him one.

Providentially—a month before Edward and Veronica died—Clout had brought Louis' mate to the reserve in a cage on the bed of his truck, exactly as Mother said he had delivered Veronica to Edward. The wedding was extravagant—I didn't want to see escargot again for a month afterward. Odetta—she adopted the name immediately—made a beautiful bride and a fetching princess.

Despite the uncertain chemistry of an arranged marriage, Louis and Odetta seemed to take to each other right off, or at least were mutually indulgent. Louis could be seen transporting mouthfuls of escargot to their nest, while Odetta swam respectfully astern Louis on their social rounds. On Swandays, before the fatal flu epidemic, the entire royal family—Edward, Veronica, Louis, Odetta and Melody—would cruise the lake crooning old favorites in five-part harmony.

I began to think of Louis and Odetta as a good match, perfectly happy, a secure cob and pen. At the Wingstrong funeral,

Odetta had been respectful and demure—a bit less so at the coronation, perhaps.

"Bloody fine-looking specimen, eh?" Father ventured to Mother.

"She's a coy one," Mother answered. "Older than him, too."

But they settled in. Louis took up the mantle of governance; Odetta assumed the social obligations of oligarchy. Father's caution seemed undue. Heeding the restoration of authority, the tundra and mute swans put a lid on their feud. I went about attending to Madeline's needs and expanding my interest in gastronomy.

Then Clout stepped in again. A month after the coronation, he took Louis to have his wings pinioned—the fate of male trumpeters at Bloedel and not at all unexpected. We saw Clout with his net in hand that morning and everyone knew what was coming—everyone, it seemed, but Louis.

Louis was returned to the marsh the next morning, a changed swan.

Even though he had never been taught to fly, losing the capacity for flight—the sudden and permanent disempowerment—must have been too much of a blow.

Outwardly the same, inwardly disfigured, for two days Louis paddled grimly from one end of the lake to the other and back again. When he finally returned to his nest, a fearful honking broke out between Louis and Odetta. It lasted all night. In the morning, a haggard Louis cast Odetta out, chasing her across the meadow in a pelting rain, she blaring in terror in the key of C major, the entire reserve watching in fascination and incredulity. Then, in a final fit of rage, Louis destroyed their nest and went straight into seclusion. You never know about relationships, Mother said—how they will stand up to trouble and what goes on in private.

The day Louis drove Odetta out, he broke all ties to his legacy and constituency. Trumpeter swans never separate. It shocked us all and was a turning point on the reserve. By that afternoon, as if ushering in a new era, a weather front had swept the sky bare—not a cloud to be seen. One didn't mind the sun now and then, actually, at least when there was a chill in the air. The dome of the sky seemed so stark that as I gazed about at our flock floating in dreamy tranquility on the lake, I tried not to imagine the devastation a new swan rivalry might bring.

"Infamy!" Father proclaimed. "There will be discord and strife until the day our king and queen are reunited."

"A bit dramatic, dear," Mother soothed, noticing the alarm in my eyes. "Royalty or commoners, newlyweds do try out their tantrums."

But Father was to be proved more right than wrong.

Being of a nervous disposition, I wished only to see our peace and stability preserved. Someone would have to step forward to take charge, I thought to myself, to protect the weak and defenseless of our community—especially me.

Edward had been regal and just, a great philosopher, admired as much as anyone with supreme authority could be. Louis just caved in. Quite frankly, not only was I fearful of what might happen without responsible leadership, I was more than a little disappointed in Louis. I'd been hopeful that in his heart he had his father's courage. But, as Mother said, pinioning had plucked his pluck. After quitting, nothing seemed to matter to him. He deserted his regular post on the lookout bluff and exiled himself to a tiny nameless island on the south side of the marsh, refusing to accept petitioners, with no one for company except a few stolid turtles.

Grimly, Louis would slide his head under a limp wing and prop himself on one leg all day long—"Like a prissy flamingo," Father remarked—or like one of the swan statues on the lawn in front of the mansion, near the fancy carved stone fountain that the jays splashed in, as if the marsh lake wasn't good enough for them, Father would also note.

It was embarrassing for Father that Louis would come to exist only as a spectacle for human visitors. Thirty feet from the island, across the narrows, there was an observation deck—roofless, with green-painted floorboards and railings. On weekends, humans would crowd the railing to view Louis. Mostly, they were respectful. Some weren't—the ones who pointed their cameras, yelled, tossed pebbles, film canisters and jellybeans to try to stir him up. But they got no response. Not long ago, Louis wouldn't have tolerated this. He would have risen up, hissing like a snake, glaring down his ebony beak, those awesome six-foot wings taut and quivering, and the humans would have drawn back, tripping over each other to escape.

At least twice a week, I would make it a point to dive for morsels near Louis' hermitage. I would swim out to the island, flip up my tail, dig into the dark green water with my orange feet and plunge—not dainty in front of a swan, I know, but it's my style and I couldn't help it. A duck is a dabbler, not a swan. "The sublime and the ridiculous," a passing crow once remarked while I was feeding a few yards from Louis. But feeding gave me a reason to be there, to try to connect with Louis, despite the rather stringy, almost indigestible aquatic tubers.

Louis didn't seem to mind this subterfuge for checking up on him. You couldn't reach him, though.

"Looks like the end of the dry spell, Louis," I remarked one morning, gagging down a tough tuber. The sky was a deepening blue with retreating wisps of high cirrus to the north, but dark rain clouds were advancing from the west. Even if you couldn't fly, it promised to be too fine an afternoon to spend with your head in a wingpit.

He brushed me off. "What is, is, Marcel." One slender, jet-black leg retracted. "What was, was." His muscular neck arched, his head snaked under a wing as white as a burst milkweed pod.

"Depression can be cured, Louis," I shouted through his feathers. "You can't live time over again once it's gone by." He'd been like this too long, going on a year. "Put your trust in nature."

"Dr. Quack." His satire wasn't muffled. "Nature is not to be trusted."

"Carpe diem, Louis!" I fired back. "You might as well be a carp!" He always put me on the defensive. Father said I was too reactive. Not a bad recovery, though. Father also said ducks are gifted with profound psychological insight. Mother said that was nonsense—such talk was just Phoenix envy.

"Stuff the philosophy," Louis said without malice. "In any case, depression is a problem of adequacy, not time."

"Have a nice day, Louis. I'm going to find something I can swallow."

"I left you a little escargot, Marcel, on the stone near the wild orchids...if they haven't slithered away by now."

I do love escargot. Mother used to bring me small servings when I was ill, the most tender of morsels. She would leave them on a lily pad and I would swish them gently in the broth of the lake before swallowing. To this day, the fragrance of escargot transports me instantly back to my early youth when I was aware only of the lush beauty of the reserve and Mother's doting, when I was ignorant of the intrigue, spite and power struggles of the world.

As different as we were, Louis and I had this in common: we were webfeet. It was a basic, genetic bond. Webfeet can share feelings and thoughts telepathically in the blink of an eye. This is how we can fly in formation. If we had to coordinate by quacks and honks, the sky would be total slapstick.

All webfeet recognize each other individually and intuitively as unique beings. This ability is important, since within our species and gender, we pretty much all look alike. As far as appearances go, a duck is a duck, a drake is a drake—in dim light, I couldn't have told Father from Uncle Arthur on a bet. Neck rings, eyes, bills, feet—all are standard issue from the Creator, all nearly identical. The physical sameness of webfeet sometimes made telling stories difficult, since you couldn't say, "Uncle Arthur squeezed up his face like Clout does when we poop on his windshield," unless, of course, Phoenix forbid, he'd been deformed by an otter attack or wounded by a hunter or tarred in an oil slick. But when I was near Uncle Arthur, I knew it was he by his webfoot aura, for lack of a better term. I kind of absorbed his entire nature all at once and knew it was my uncle and no one else.

In a dense gathering, however, it wasn't always easy to know with whom you were conversing. Strong personalities crowded in on you. I had more than once addressed Uncle Arthur as "Father" because Father was floating right behind me. Not only that, you could be chatting with a charming duck, suddenly realize she had the personality of a drake, and then have to hide your confusion as you carefully scanned the area to see whose "he" it was that you were engaged with—the duck in front of you, a nearby drake, or perhaps a nearby ventriloquist playing a joke. I get confused even trying to explain this.

Father said it was the life goal of a drake to find his drakehood and let it be known through his aura, loud and clear to the world. "Just between you and me, son, it's often difficult to detect your presence," he told me. "Something you need to work on, Marcel—a big presence." But Father's expectations always made me feel even smaller.

Acts of generosity were not uncommon among webfeet. The tundras allowed Odetta to live with them—except during mating season, naturally. We had all politely welcomed the mute swans—that chichi Euro crowd, as Father called them, noting how they curved their necks, orange bills always pointing down in disdain—even after they deigned to make their winter visits permanent, posing a threat to the tundras. And we tolerated the formations of rowdy Canada geese that flocked in seasonally, fouling the grass for five months and leaving us with the mess. They understood us and we understood them, I liked to think. We were all webfeet. It was the web that connected us. "Birds of a feather flock together" doesn't quite get it. It should be something like, "Toes tied, souls allied." But that sounds too much like "soles"—ah, well, I never was a poet, like Louis.

Unfortunately, our history proved that sameness could sometimes breed discord. The smallest differences could end up in the biggest conflicts. And like all the Creator's creatures, we were territorial. Plus, we all had our own religious beliefs, about the exact nature of the Almighty, and especially about the afterlife—who got to go to heaven and so forth. But I'm getting ahead of myself again.

As a fellow webfoot, Louis' isolation was all the more difficult to understand and bear for me. During his brief reign he became somewhat aloof, as leaders must. But until Clout came for him he was in our midst daily, and, with his beautiful evening concerts, brought us together — separation and broken relationships being the worst kind of pain.

Yet another separation was to follow. My brother Troy was the alpha male in our brood, a born leader, his speculum brightest, his grunt sharp with authority. As a duckling, he was inspired to action by the vast serpentines of migratory flocks that swept beneath the sun—north in spring, south in autumn—making the light flicker from dawn to dusk. As soon as he was old enough to mate, Troy departed the reserve to command the first migration of Bloedel mallards in two generations. "Phoenix speed," Mother called with tears of pride and sadness as Troy's flock launched from the marsh in a thunder of wings and heroic quacks, frothing the lake white.

In admiration and, frankly, a bit of suppressed envy, I watched the voyagers circle overhead as they organized into a wavy V, my brother at the point, his new mate, Belle, just aft his right wing, abeam her brother Nick.

Nick had contended with Troy for leadership, finally deferring, albeit sullenly, at the behest of his newlywed sister. Formed up, the flock wheeled south, driving into the hazy autumn sun, their rallying cries lapsing fainter and fainter. I wasn't to see Troy again until just before Father was killed. And my next encounter with Belle and Nick — no, I'm sorry, this is too much to tell at once. Mother said that the purpose of a story is to stretch weird events apart far enough to insert narrative credibility.

Chapter 3

"Blasphemy, sacrilege!" Father sputtered. "To take the sign of the Phoenix in vain like that—typical of a barbaric human." Newly painted on Clout's mailbox was a gilded emblem of a great bird with outstretched wings.

"It's an eagle, dear," Mother said. "No one has ever seen the Phoenix."

When Father got really worked up, he thrashed the water with his bill. "Nonsense, of course they have." He churned the surface like a waterspout. "Paranoid, that Clout. Witness, please, this pernicious compulsion of his to pinion trumpeter swans—insane possessiveness, if you ask any rational being. If I were a trumpeter I wouldn't put up with it." He glanced at Mother, who had hopped onto the bank. "Where are you going, Doris?"

"Just moving into the shade, dear." Mother answered, "The sun is too bright."

Father didn't follow her. He didn't like to be on dry land, where the metal band on his leg was exposed to view. The band was a stigma, and the banded were derided by those who had so far escaped Clout's interest—meaning his net. The tundras were especially merciless, sending Father rowdy, contemptuous bleats whenever they spied him out of the water, lunching on fresh green shoots in the meadow. Although I would never have dared to share this with Father, a little sparkle on the leg could be quite attractive, I thought, and quite harmless. Tempted, despite the risk of Father's wrath, I sometimes paddled too near when I saw Clout row out in his red canoe, net in hand.

"On Judgment Day, all will have to confront the Phoenix," Father said, "including Clout and the tundras."

Piety was central to life on the reserve. Citizens depended on signs and symbols to help make decisions. They looked to our spiritual guides for interpretation and to do the negotiating with the Creator, since such portentous things as cloud shapes and ripples in the water were so complex and abundant that their meanings were not always evident, at least not to me—or if they were obvious, no one knew what to do next. For example, one morning a cloud appeared on the horizon that looked like a huge otter. Everyone was jumpy until evening, long after the shape had lost definition and drifted away. Another time, a huge webbed foot washed up on the shore, resulting in a disturbing rumor that the Phoenix had been caught by an otter, until someone pointed out that the foot was made of orange rubber, had a buckle on the back, and was obviously a human prosthesis.

There were quite a few guides and gurus to choose from. One was a magpie named Pica-Pica living in the old pines. He specialized in pond ripples. He would make a low pass and drop a couple of small holy tokens—or sometimes escargot shells if he was short of tokens—onto the glassy surface of a pool. Where the objects hit, ripples spread out in circles from the little splashes. How the ripples intersected was supposed to tell the future. "This is truth, not superstition," Pica-Pica would shout, puffing up his black-and-white feathers when a potential client hesitated. "The entire universe works this way—a ying splash and a yang splash, a good splash and an evil splash, two rings of waves from the future converging, passing through each other. Being gifted, I alone can say what events the waves will bring to us, to you, my friend." The previous year he advised his third cousin to diversify her nest eggs, which she took as encouragement to copulate with him, causing no end of family grief.

Another sage, Jerome, an impatient jay, would listen to your question, drop a pine cone on one side of the culvert, then flit across the road to see which way it was pointing as it floated out the other side. "Come on, come on!" he would screech into the end of the big pipe.

Frankly, though, just when you need it the most is when advice can be most confusing. Mother always said to be careful whom you trust—that most mystics are quacks if not plain cuckoo. Father once paid Jerome a substantial sum in crow quills to have his leg band removed. Jerome's vigorous incantations attracted the interest of an otter, which Father barely escaped in a frantic, splashing take-off. Jerome was unapologetic, claiming that the otter was under his spell and would have stripped off the band if only Father hadn't fled. "If I could find those quills, I'd take them all back," Father complained ruefully to Mother.

For a long while, not quills, but tabs—the silver tabs from the cans that human visitors drank from—had been our currency. These were traded on the flock market. Magpies, as our bankers, collected tokens by the hundreds—shamelessly, Father would complain, his bill thrashing the water, "without any purpose except to hoard for themselves." But as the number of visitors increased, any bird could pick tabs off the ground before the magpies got to them. Having lost their scarcity, inflation set in and the tabs became almost worthless. It took hundreds just to pay for a single prayer. So we switched to quills, the denominations depending on scarcity, molting cycles and social rank. The most precious quills naturally were from trumpeter swans. It is said that Edward and Veronica were stripped to bare flesh even before the buzzards got to them.

At Bloedel, two religions were mainstream. On one wing were those who worshiped the Phoenix—the mute swans, we ducks and all the perchers.

On the other wing was the Horus congregation—the tundra swans, the geese and the soaring birds.

Phoenix and Horus were believed to be part god and part bird. It was believed that they had the power to regulate entry into heaven, depending on the applicant's behavior in life—which was monitored from hatching to expiration.

I often wished there were no heaven, so that we wouldn't have to be treated as so expendable on earth. I would be quite content to be simply discontinued, so to speak, at some point, and fondly remembered by family and friends. Of course, it would be icing on the drake to perpetuate some remnant of myself, in the form of a brood of little ducklings — which Madeline and I would eventually, we prayed, hatch together. Confronting immortality seemed too huge an undertaking for an individual bird to deal with. I had never cultivated many interests apart from food and easily found myself bored after only a few hours of inactivity, let alone for all eternity.

Frankly, choosing between one god or the other seemed speculative at best, although I would never have said so to Father. Both religions predicted a Judgment Day, when the world would be burnt to a crisp, Phoenix or Horus swooping in to rescue their respective faithful just in time—something worth considering, I must admit, if this were expected within one's lifetime. Pica-Pica once erroneously foretold the day of the final conflagration and Father had almost died of anxiety by evening. Pica-Pica evaded him for a month afterward.

In addition to Phoenixism and Horusanity, there were several fringe beliefs on the reserve, such as Owlism, an arcane, scholarly, monolithic faith, that claimed to be the most ancient, and kept mostly to itself. Its followers rolled an egg out of a nest every full moon, examining the residue for the secrets that created a fully formed bird.

Religious rivalry between the tundra and mute swans often erupted into rowdy hissing-and-honking arguments that could be heard across the reserve, a sad reflection, Father said, on webfoot diplomacy. But the trumpeters always managed to calm things down before any real violence started. Trumpeter swans were theologically neutral, if not inscrutable, siding with neither the Phoenix nor Horus, the mute swans nor the tundras, an impartiality that Mother said had helped raise them to leadership.

"One generally worships whom one was brought up to worship," Louis said one night, a full moon seeming to drain his brilliant white form of all heat, "until one can make up one's own mind. The lake does not choose to reflect the swan, the swan does not choose to be reflected by the lake."

"Pure and simple frogwash," Father retorted, almost choking on a tendril, when I proudly repeated this hearsay at breakfast. "Doesn't bloody matter, excuse my language, what a bird *thinks*. When you are gripped by The Response, why, that's it—you must surrender to the Phoenix, you *have* to obey, you have no choice." His sleek blue-green head seemed to glow and his white neck ring throbbed as he fixed me with a hard stare. "No other choice, that is, but to go to Hell, son."

"Such glorious plumage, the Phoenix," Mother put in, "that's how I imagine him—all gold and emerald and vermilion, like a peacock, like amour shining in the sun."

"Armor, Doris," Father corrected, dunking his head feathers into the lake to achieve more of a gloss.

The Response is a certain thing that was supposed to happen to you sometime in life where you and the Phoenix became intimately involved with each other, something like Madeline and I felt when we first mated, but apparently much more intense. In fact, the Phoenix was supposed to take control of you, or you were supposed to allow it to. It was a kind of surrender. Father was very dedicated to this idea. He took us to services on Swandays to hear the story of how, long ago, the Almighty, enchanted by what he believed his most perfect creation, used to stop his sky chariot every day to listen to the Phoenix sing.

It was really quite a gripping story, especially when told by our pastor, Jasper, a convincing red-naped sapsucker who promoted himself a cardinal. The original Phoenix, like all birds that didn't suffer a fatal accident or illness, eventually got old and feeble and near to death. Since there was only one Phoenix, death would also have put to rest the entire species—apparently there's never been a Mrs. Phoenix to lay some eggs. However, the Almighty, realizing how much He would miss His daily serenade, devised an ingenious method—not to condescend to the Almighty, here, of course—to carry on the Phoenix line with only a male to work with. It must be more economical to make new birds than to keep patching up old ones.

According to Pastor Jasper, each time the Phoenix felt his death approaching he built himself a nest of a particular aromatic cedar. Then he set the nest on fire, and when the heat became intense and the wood began to crackle and sigh, he jumped into the flames and burned to ashes. Bang!—a brand new Phoenix sprang from the smoldering pyre. Quite amazing, really—much more dramatic than a molt. My brother Harold thought Clout was mixed up in the process—in winter, anyway, when smoke poured out of his chimney—but we watched for months and never saw the Phoenix pop out.

Harold and I would also watch airplanes passing high over the reserve, trailing thin tracks of white smoke and shaking the marsh with a dull thunder.

"The Phoenix watches us from on high," Father would say in a portentous tone, always trying to galvanize our faith.

One day two planes appeared in the sky together going in opposite directions.

"Must be some kind of optical illusion," Father sputtered.

Anyway, this self-immolation by the Phoenix was distinctly different from the normal sexual reproduction we were familiar with on the reserve, but it did have the merit of speed and simplicity, I supposed. And—I am guessing here—the new Phoenix got to hang on to who he was, to keep his old self, memories and all. The worst part about death seems to be having to give up who you are, or to quit trying to be who you thought you wanted to be before you are ready.

"You see, the Phoenix doesn't need to bother at all about a mate and raising a family, Doris," Father said. "He is immortal and bloody well worth worshipping."

This seemed to distress Mother—the down of her graceful mottled brown breast ruffled and I floated myself closer to comfort her.

Father sidestepped the thing about the Phoenix burning up every so many years. I used to wish the Phoenix would stop by the reserve and talk about this, like how painful it was. I wondered what he did all day, guessing he spent a lot of time keeping heaven shipshape. Actually, I hoped the Phoenix would drop in at the reserve to help solve our leadership crisis before it got out of hand and draconian measures were required. I was sure it wouldn't have taken more than a few minutes out of his schedule. Perhaps he was simply unaware of the situation. Someone needed to go and get him.

Quite a few of the more intellectual birds had no use at all for religion. They kept to themselves in a professional society—the aviary tower crowd, father called them—making all kinds of plans to improve our chances of survival. Using scientific research, their main project was to fly to the moon, thus escaping any future scourges that might destroy the reserve. Their leader was a rook named Caruthers. "You can wait until the crows come home for your savior," he said to Father. "When calamity strikes, only those who are prepared will survive."

"What absurdity," Father retorted. "How many birds do you think are going to fit on the lunar surface? Maybe two perchers at the most on a full moon, no more than one little finch on a quarter, even if one of us could fly there, which I very much doubt. I myself have migrated from Vancouver Island and I can tell you it is not a drake-walk. The moon must be at least twice the distance."

It always surprised me how many opinions there could be about a subject and how hard it was to judge which was truth. "We are all the same underneath our feathers," Pastor Jasper, flitting back and forth between two branches of an oak, once told us in a sermon. "We must cease our constant searching for differences. It can only lead to dissent and spiritual breakdown, turning brother against brother, kin against kin." He concluded with a sharp whistle. "Now, the rain has left us refreshments in the meadow, for those of you who appreciate a good mushroom. Mind that you avoid the poisonous jack o' lanterns, which except for the gills can appear identical to the chanterelles."

Mother was not very curious about religion and had no interest at all in science. She was more of a historian than a theologian. Each evening, ever since we were ducklings, she related the history of the reserve to her broods—chapter upon chapter, whether amid the summer fragrance of hyacinths or the stinging winter hail. We listened enthralled—at least I would—as we sheltered for the night off the lee bank of our section of the lake. In soothing murmurs—more for emotional impact than information, since she relied on webfoot telepathy to communicate with us—Mother shared her remembrances and the legends passed down from her family.

After Madeline and I were mated, I would bring her to listen, except when there were eggs to be sat on, of course, or when she had a headache. For some reason, our eggs never hatched. Madeline would lay a batch, but long after a normal incubation period, they would still be eggs. Eventually, we would have to push them out of the nest and watch them roll down the bank into the lake. They didn't sink, of course, and in the morning we would have to face five or six half-submerged eggs floating in the cove, sometimes for days, until the wind or a current drew them out into the lake, to be devoured by otters or other creatures. Madeline would sink into deep depression each time and no matter how much I tried to comfort her it would be weeks before she bounced back. "Let's tidy up this nest, Marcel," she would say, finally, "and give the neighbors one less thing to talk about." It was in our nature to keep trying. In desperation, she would sometimes swim in behind another duck whose little yellow ducklings were trailing behind, hoping to attract and lure away a few laggards—to adopt them, sort of. But after an hour she would return them, and my heart would break with love for her.

Mother's chronicle of our reserve became far more interesting to me than anything I could imagine in my own dull future. Moreover, I had grown to depend on her storytelling. Those nightly bedtime stories brought comfort, the antidote to my agitation and insomnia. "A mama's boy," Father said, and it was true, I admit. If she were to miss a night, I believed I could not have fallen asleep at all. The slightest rustle of cattails and I would see in the shadows a posse of nocturnal gourmand otters slipping into the water, preparing to grab my legs and pull me under.

The first night that Louis came to visit—I was still a duckling—there was a big fuss as Mother prepared our nest for this royal guest. Father sent us off early to our sleeping spot. I stayed awake almost until dawn, or so it seemed, waiting desperately for Mother as the moon cradled itself across the sky, its reflection shimmying in the black lake, slipping occasionally behind silver-edged clouds, then emerging again to reveal our flock frozen in slumber like hundreds of decoys—all in slumber but me, that is. The crickets and frogs announced their lusty intentions, interrupted by an occasional crackle in the underbrush that would for an instant halt their chants and also my heart.

At last Louis departed and Mother came to nuzzle me goodnight. "No story tonight, dear," she said, "it's too late." It was the first time I had been denied a goodnight story. I was angry and hurt, furious with Louis for making me stew in my fears and anxieties for all those hours. When finally I did sink into sleep, a frightening dream took stage before me.

The morning sky hung red like dripping blood. An otter pursued me. I tried to escape. I flapped with all my strength but gravity chained me to the water as if my wings were pinioned and my feet stone. I could only drag my belly along the surface, leaving a frothing trail for the otter to follow. Alert to my helplessness, the otter closed in, aiming hard down the bubbling funnel of my wake. I could hear its snorts behind my tail, smell its musk, taste Phoebe's blood in the water. My wing roots in searing pain, my will exhausted, I was on the verge of quitting, to have it over with. Suddenly, I felt a surge of energy from below, an upward shove. I was lifted off the marsh as if by other wings, inch by inch away from the snapping jaws beneath my feet. I gained altitude. I looked down. A mallard thrashed in the grip of an otter. A red stain spread out from them. Then the otter was gone, the marsh was gone. I had risen not into the blood red sky or even the familiar air above the reserve but into some other sky above some other land.

Chapter 4

Absent trumpeter governance, tension between rival flocks began to tear apart our society. The threat of otters paled in comparison to the possible onset of civil war. Skirmishes on the disputed border between the tundra and mute swans flared up daily, jarring the air with furious honks. I was dozing on a bank one pleasant afternoon, a light drizzle roughing up the surface of the lake and making the water lilies tremble the way I liked, when Cyrus, the tundra chief, escorted by three of his airborne troops, suddenly swooped in to attack a wood duck who had strayed into their territory the previous day. The soldiers pecked at him, jabbing hard. When he tried to escape, they pursued him a good thirty yards into a grove of ferns, their long necks thrusting forward, their beaks agape and spitting, stiff black tongues protruding like little vipers.

"Phoenix infidel!" Cyrus hissed. "Keep with your own."

You could feel his rage ripple out in waves as if a stone had been dropped into a deep pool of hatred. Witnessing such viciousness inflicted on a fellow duck opened the wound in my heart from Phoebe's death and I uttered an involuntary grunt. My feet actually took a few sympathetic steps in the direction of the victim, drawing the attention of one of the attackers, who shot me a fierce warning glance. My lame gesture must have inspired the victim, though. He had a lot of pluck. Regaining his footing, eyes blazing, quacking fiercely, he lunged at Cyrus's henchmen, and they gave him some berth. You have to stand up to bullies, Father always said, and here was an example. It made me proud to be a duck—yet renewed the shame of hesitance.

The mute swans retaliated the next day. Alexander, their chief, led a reprisal of five warbirds, diving out of the sun on a hapless, quite innocent young gander.

"You and your militant goose-stepping goons," Alexander taunted him. "We are not intimidated."

Severely injured, unable to fly, the goose hobbled back home, routed his mate out of their nest, and punctured all their eggs. "I'm not bringing goslings into a world like this," he screeched.

And so it went, vigilante attacks on the blameless, day after day. Talk on the reserve spoke of open warfare. The tundra and mute swans were conducting regular aerial formation and marching drills.

"You must do something, Marcel," Madeline said. "I'm afraid."

Worry for her safety sent my digestive system out of kilter, my standard response to an urgent demand for action. My feathers looked haggard. I decided I had to seek help. I would consult our wisest, most respected birds.

"What can be done?" I asked Father.

"Evil, these Horus hoodlums, Marcel—not to fret yourself, though," he counseled. "The reserve seems to be going to hell in an egg basket, I know, but we must keep strong in our faith."

"It's never really been quite this violent, though, Basil," Mother said.

Father stirred the water gently. "All is well, dear," he soothed, "the Phoenix will come at the appropriate time, as it is foretold on the Stump and Bark."

The Stump and Bark were the sacred repositories of the entire history, prophesy and sacraments of Phoenixism. The Stump was the remains of a huge redwood tree felled in the woods south of the mansion. Pastor Jasper said the Almighty had planted the tree at the beginning of time and that it was holy. He could read the entire history of the world from the Stump's rings. "Here's where the Almighty created the first immortal bird—the Phoenix," he would edify us, pecking lightly at a ring midway from the center of the Stump. "And here is where the Phoenix appointed us cardinals to be his permanent apostles."

"Far as I can tell, Jasper, you're still a sapsucker," Uncle Arthur advised.

The Bark was a long, dried peel of white birch bark covered with arcane markings. It was kept in the hollow of an ancient oak. As interpreted by Pastor Jasper, this parchment told our future all the way out to Judgment Day. The Bark also prescribed in detail all moral conduct and behavior required of the Phoenix faithful, as well as the punishments for disobedience. The central code of the Bark was a list of rules called the Holy Presentments. Father lived by these.

"Father," I asked, "couldn't we somehow try to bring Cyrus and Alexander together to seek a truce?"

"You would compromise Phoenixism, Marcel?" He gave me an incredulous blink, paddled backward a good yard and thrashed the water with his bill. "Why, you can't trust mutes as far as you can throw them. They're unspeakable idolaters, son. When it comes to our Alexander versus their Cyrus, it's saint versus devil. If you know the Bark, you only have to think of the First Presentment, 'Root out an idolater as you would a tick.' The Phoenix will deal with all pagans and idolaters, son, you can count on it. The day of reckoning is coming for those that worship Horus."

"But Father," I protested, "the swans aren't so different. Why do they hate each other? What is there to resent about any of them?" Or any other bird, I wondered, but didn't say, knowing how Father felt about jays.

"It isn't given to us to know everything, son," he said, his irises beginning to shimmer. "Not in this world, but we will know all in the life to come."

That didn't sound like much to look forward to. One of my great pleasures has always been to feel a sense of wonder and mystery about the universe—to let waves of awe sweep over me as I gazed at the clouds, the misty bulk of Mount Rainier in the distance, the spring flowers, the stars at night, realizing how little I could comprehend. In the next world, I would know everything, how it all worked, why things happened the way they did, and nothing would be mysterious. On the surface, it promised to be frightfully boring in Heaven, with nothing left to find out.

"I just don't understand why they hold these grudges, Father," I said.

"You have much to learn in the world, Son," he said. "A grudge can be a useful way to fill the time, to help keep evil under control while we wait for the Phoenix to come. It's a force that holds everything together." He leveled a fatherly gaze at me and I felt naïve, as I often did in his presence. "Yes, a great force, Marcel, that doesn't lose power even over generations."

I tried to imagine grudges as a kind of music, the way a song can fill time. As they say, music soothes the savage beak. I liked music. In fact, I imagined music dissolving time, the way raindrops disappear in the lake. Listening to the songbirds at dawn and dusk—most of all the trumpeters, before they went silent—brought me hours of carefree pleasure. As for my own abilities, I could grunt out a decent rhythm—more of a steady panting, really—but when it came to trilling a melody, well, although we have pleasant, reedy voices, a duck isn't so blessed in that department. For someone like me, though, music cuts out a lot of idle, not to say wasteful, cogitation. "Thinking too much isn't always healthy, Marcel," Mother would counsel, "just trust your instincts, dear." Indeed, a good aria could always put me in touch with my deeper feelings.

But grudges and music seemed out of harmony.

I considered approaching Louis about the civil unrest. Considering Father's certainty of the prophecy of the Bark—that the Phoenix would arrive to halt the march to war—I hesitated. It might seem a betrayal of trust in Father.

"What do you think?" I asked Madeline. I had explained the situation in careful detail. As my mate, I respected her opinion almost as much as Mother's, but of course I couldn't ask Mother about Father.

"Think about what, Marcel?" We had been mated less than a year and were still perfecting our communications.

"Whether I should simply accept Father's advice," I summarized, "and leave it at that."

Madeline paddled by, her beak trailing two long, dried reeds. She was still busy with the finishing touches of buttressing our nest. She always spoke expectantly of our future broods.

"Aren't you going to help me with this, Marcel?" she asked.

I looked around for some twigs.

"Advice about what?" she asked.

She was clearly preoccupied. "It's not important, dear," I said.

"You'll let me know first, won't you, Marcel." she said, turning to face me, the reeds still hanging from her beak.

"Let you know?"

"You won't just go off and do something—no matter what I said."

"Of course not, dear," I said, startled, "only to speak with Louis." What did she mean? I couldn't imagine that I would go off anywhere to do anything. With my weak constitution and irritable gizzard, the least upset would incapacitate me for days. Once, Madeline had been stricken after a luncheon at which she'd eaten an odd variety of slug. She'd retched for an hour. Nearly insane with anxiety, I'd flapped all about the reserve looking for medical help. All the practitioners were away at a tournament, but fortunately Madeline's stomach settled down by itself. The point is, I would always look for someone else to step in. The next morning, Madeline said that she'd only wanted me to stay by her side for reassurance. "It was only a bilious stomach, Marcel," she said, comforting *me*. "You were very sweet, though, chasing all about."

I decided to consult with Louis. Father would not be offended, I reasoned, since he respected Louis' heritage, if not his courage. Father was loyal to the memory of Edward.

I hadn't visited Louis for over a week. Impatient, I decided to fly directly to the island rather than paddle there on my usual meandering route, feigning a chance encounter. I always felt guilty when Louis would see me flying. I wanted us to be on equal terms. But now, perhaps to steel myself against his gloom, I chose to savor my wings.

I flapped up high above the tallest pines, nearly touching the flat, gray bases of some scattered white clouds. There I circled, sucking in cool, damp air, trying to organize my thoughts. A hawk orbited nearby, waiting for something tasty to scoot out into the open. Below me, the island, on which stood visible a single white berry on a stem—our abdicated king.

I would try to take my time broaching the subject of my visit, drawing Louis out slowly, as the robins pull worms from the ground. He wouldn't be forthcoming, I knew that.

Swooshing in to land feet first, I sent a playful spray of water onto the bank, where Louis stood frozen in his one-legged pose, head tucked under a wing, feathers ruffling in the light breeze. Anemic ripples lapped the shore. The puffy clouds skimmed by in perfect silence. Behind Louis, yellow butterflies danced in the mottled light beneath a young birch. A stand of cattails leaned slightly as if to comfort him. A dozen or so escargot shells lay scattered about, testifying that not all Louis's links to royalty had been severed—at least not the gastronomical one. The visitors' deck across from the island stood empty, save for one woman wearing a blue dress and straw hat, peering at Louis through binoculars.

"Good morning, Louis," I offered, still a little breathless from flight.

"A fly-in breakfast today, Marcel? Most unusual for you, a change in routine—signifying what, I wonder?" Many birds were put off by Louis's affected tone, but to me it was his defense against his shyness.

"The otters are out and about," I said. "Good idea to keep the feet out of the water." My conscience always winced at lies—I expected the woman with the binoculars to announce that she hadn't noticed any otters in the area.

"Have I ever told you, Marcel, how I enjoy your little visits to my island?"

"No, Louis," I answered, taken aback. I have to admit that I often regarded myself as a boring sycophant, whom Louis tolerated only for the flattery.

"Don't get me wrong," he said, "it's not that I don't savor my solitude, free to be alone in my thoughts, but one does have to contend with the monotonous passage of time. How it moves inexorably in a straight line, you know."

"I enjoy your company, too, Louis," I said truthfully. I was beginning to fidget, wanting to get to the purpose of my visit.

"Time that moves in a straight line can induce the notion that something nasty awaits at the end of it," he said. "There is a certain threat in the steady passage of time—you know what I mean, Marcel?"

I didn't.

Louis's head slowly withdrew from under his wing. "The unknown future looming up at one—unless one is busy with something, some business to engage in," he said. Behind his eyes you could almost see thoughts flickering like a pool of tadpoles in sunlight. "On the other wing, time that travels in a circle, Marcel, is rejuvenating, quite reviving."

I hadn't the faintest idea what time going in a straight line was, or in a circle, or in a zig-zag, or even what ordinary time was, for that matter. You woke up, you went to sleep. In between, time brought you beauty, pain and an amazing variety of problems with other birds and beings. As long as you were living in time, you were surrounded by worry—like ripples when you swam—about what time would bring to you.

Actually, time brought you everything except food—you had to go after that yourself.

"Time in a circle," Louis repeated. "The very crux of religion, you know—rebirth, heaven—all that sort of thing, how you can come round in a big loop and wipe the past clean, how time circles back again for us when it reaches its end, like a trained falcon in his gyre or a homing pigeon, bless their neurotic hearts."

The conversation was so confusing that I was afraid I would forget what I had come for. "Things are really getting out of control on the reserve, Louis," I blurted.

"The falcon, of course, to his credit, sometimes doesn't return. But, ah!…the purpose of your visit today, Marcel, what you really came to discuss…let's see, was it how to swim with the feet out of the water? A back float, as it were—most ungainly and undignified for a duck, upside down with the head submerged. No, perhaps you wished to discuss something to do with…my mute and tundra kin?"

I should have known he had already read my mind.

"Yes."

"That is not my problem, my friend."

"If the fighting escalates, it will affect us all, even you on your island."

"Things will only go so far, Marcel."

"How can you say that?" It was amazing how a bird could balance so long on one leg. "We're on the brink of war."

Louis looked at me squarely. "Clout," he said in a level tone.

"What about Clout?"

"He'll step in. He controls all."

"Louis," I protested, "Clout can't control the swans."

"Look what he did to me."

Louis strained to spread his wings, but the effort only produced a tremble that seemed to pass through his torso and ripple down his leg. With that, it finally became clear to me: Louis was in love with his pain. Friendship can blind you to such obvious facts for a long time.

"You've suffered a great loss, Louis," I said, making ready to leave, but willing to give what he wanted — some sympathy.

"I used to get angry for feeling sorry for myself, Marcel—about losing the wings, you know—all that self-pity for months on end. So I finally decided to quit lamenting what can't be undone. But then I felt empty. I missed the grieving, the sadness itself, and I realized there's no end to the sorrows one can have, if one desires them—my parents, Odetta, the entire pitiful state of the reserve, for that matter. I'd like to help you, Marcel, but I'm quite stuck here. I'd be lost without my sorrows."

I felt an overwhelming urge to get away, as when sitting with someone dying slowly with the flu, hearing the chest fill up. Actually, I noticed that Louis was sounding a bit wheezy. "I'll be going, now, Louis," I said.

"And it's time you stopped patronizing me, Marcel—unbecoming for both of us. You're a natural diplomat. Float tall."

I stared at him, my bill agape.

"Speak to the tundra and mute leaders, Marcel."

"What!" I quacked. "Me?"

"Cyrus and Alexander hate each other but neither will risk war until he's confident of winning. Find something to offer them—another way out, so they can save face."

My wings felt heavy as logs. My stomach began to churn. It was beyond my ability to resolve a dispute between two goldfinches over a thistle seed, let alone warlords over a reserve.

"You may need credentials." Louis reached back and plucked a long white quill from his left wing—wrenched it out, really, with a hard twist that must have been agonizing. Reaching back again, he tore an identical pinion from the other wing. "Quite useless, now," he said, "but they'll know where these came from. They still fear me."

Staring at the disembodied quills, I wondered how much Cyrus and Alexander still feared Louis.

Louis closed his eyes and concentrated hard for a moment, and in the distance I heard the faint but unmistakable blare of a trumpeter swan. "That was my sister, Melody. She nests on the far north bank. If you ever need help, Marcel, go to her."

The woman on the deck was still training her binoculars our way when I saw her shift slightly. Clout was rounding the island in his red canoe. He drifted past us without a glance, one last stroke pivoting the canoe alongside the deck. An animated conversation ensued between Clout, one hand against the deck to steady himself, and the woman—both of them squeezing their faces, baring teeth and gesticulating gracelessly the way humans do. Clout made a sound like a crow discovering fresh road kill, almost tipping over the boat, and the woman rejoined with a sort of hawk cry, high pitched and feverish. Then the woman sat down on the edge of the deck and lowered herself abruptly into the canoe, grabbing Clout's free hand. As the boat started to rock, their faces contorted, their eyes bulged. The woman let out a shriek and her hand seized Clout's shirt like a talon. The canoe rolled and water spilled over the gunwales, but it finally settled down and Clout pushed off from the deck, picked up his paddle and brought the bow around. As they drew closer, I could see that under her hat the woman's head fur was as amber as a day-old duckling. This time, Clout looked our way. The woman pointed at Louis, her teeth bared but her face bright and relaxed. Clout dug in with the paddle and the canoe scooted around the island.

"See how she pointed at you, Louis?" I said. "You're a trumpeter swan—to be admired and envied."

"They're planning something else for me," Louis said, his head already hidden under his wing.

Chapter 5

After a restless night, I blinked awake to a sluggish dawn. Fog cast a gray sheen across the marsh, the air close and clinging like cobwebs. Except for the regular hoot of an owl, I was ensconced in perfect silence. My throat was dry and I felt a need to gargle but couldn't—Louis' wing quills were still clamped in my bill.

I felt a presence.

Not a wingspan away floated Troy, emaciated, ragged, his head feathers and speculum muted to a turbid gray by the weak light.

Before I could utter a word, I felt him hush me. "Don't wake anyone, Marcel."

"Troy, you're back!" I blurted, anyway, the quills dropping into the water, my voice a parched rasp.

"Why the hell are you sleeping with swan feathers in your mouth?" Troy whispered, as I snatched them back.

Realizing the quills had floated, I spit them out again and took a quick gargle from the lake, trying to speak at the same time. "Great Phoenix, Troy!" I choked. "What happened to you?" I could see now that his left eye was shut, making him look like one of our night perimeter guards, who sleep with one eye open. I rushed to him, extending a wing across his back, smoothing down his feathers, wanting to embrace. I felt a tingling of joy all over my skin, my down fluffing up as if it were winter.

"Easy, Marcel, easy," he said, backing off. My brother was never one for drake-to-drake contact. He smelled a bit of fermentation—tartly sweet and sour.

But perhaps my touch had been painful to him. Back-paddling, I started to say, "Your eye, Troy…"

"Just a little souvenir," he interrupted. "The other one still works fine."

"Souvenir?"

"It's a cruel world, Marcel, he said. "Count your blessings." He edged closer, glancing at Louis' quills, which had drifted a few wingspans away. "Listen, I understand that Pastor Jasper still offers private consultations—I've been away a long time, been through a lot, as you can tell, and could use a little spiritual propping up, so to say. But he charges a fee and frankly I haven't got a thing to my name at the moment save the feathers on my back."

"Troy?" It was Mother. "Troy, is it you?"

In one heartbeat, a burst of joy exploded from Mother, our entire flock jolted instantly to life around us—a ruckus of wings and quacks and spray. Some ducks took to the air, believing we were under attack. Others skidded on their feet to shore, wings beating, to protect nests.

"But look at you!" Mother exclaimed. "Emaciated!" Propped erect by her beating wings, she hovered above Troy, a shield to protect him. "Marcel," she beckoned. "Bring Troy something to eat—a slug, something nutritional. Just look at him! Where has he been? Basil, look, it's Troy!"

While our family and flock pressed in on Troy, all quacking at once, I went in search of a slug. I would find time with my brother later.

Slugs were not all that easy to see in the dimly lit long grass, and it took me a while to find a good fat one, having first to eat three inferior specimens, rather than let them go to waste.

By the time I returned with the slug in my bill, Troy had been ushered to our nest by Madeline and made to settle in for a rest. Madeline conveyed the slug the last few feet from me to Troy, quacking excessively, as broodless ducks do when their nurturing hormones are stimulated.

Then, I thought, "The quills!"

I rushed to the spot near the submerged log where I sleep, but, of course, Louis' quills were no longer to be seen. I felt my gizzard sink. Phoenix only knew where they could have floated off to.

In a panic, I launched from the lake, leveled off at the treetops and commenced a systematic search, starting at our sleeping cove and spiraling out, the whole time fretting and rebuking myself for my birdbrain irresponsibility. I was glad I hadn't yet told Father about the quills. "Marcel, you'd forget your tail if it wasn't stuck to your butt," he'd pronounce, shaking his head.

As I circled, I realized I should have immediately hidden the quills in the brush. Instead, I'd waited until the sun had set to return to the flock, hoping no one would notice the white plumage in my bill; among ducks, sudden quirky behavior can arouse suspicions of debility and untrustworthiness. Before I could devise a short, plausible account of the quills, I'd returned to our cove and found myself floating next to my brother Harold at Mother's story time.

"Trés chichi, Marcel," Harold had cooed in mock approval. Mother, about to begin her narration, had sent me a glance of welcome, which, when she saw the long white quills dangling from my bill, transformed into dismay, followed by a shrug of her wings as she'd cleared her throat for the story.

Widening my spiral, I scanned the lake—the broad shallows with its clumps of reeds, the overgrown banks, flotsam, anywhere the quills might have lodged. After more than two hours, nothing. The air was still calm, but the fog was burning off and the sun was painting a fiery band along the eastern horizon, promising a breeze later, if not a storm, which would chase feathers afar.

There, a white quill! Like a pelican above a mackerel, I tucked wings and fell. The water came up too fast. I snapped open my wings to brake, my shoulders taking a terrific jerk, prepared myself to hit the water, and—right there! Snout! Black eyes! Ripply shape!

Squawk!—feet slap water, brush whiskers, bump snout, jowl, teeth—wings pump for dear life, lungs heave, heart thuds—lumbering duck body slung low, dead weight—right wingtip down! dipping into water, don't flip over!—everything slowing down, the world in slow motion, time coming to a stop—the world frozen!

Death.

No—released, moving again, climbing at last, into the orange sun—faster, senses alive, scanning—blur of poplars to the left, smell of dead carp, smoke from Clout's chimney, two high-up blackbirds harassing a hawk, bright music from the mansion windows.

Safe, safe—nothing compares with escape.

Shaking, ripped between impulses—snatch Louis' quill before it gets away! flee home, to nest, to Madeline!—I strain for height, up, into the haven of the sky.

I circled the marsh, calming down, flapping less, gliding more, letting my pulse slow, the sharp ache in my shoulders fade, the grip of fear relax, my fractured cosmos come together.

The universe had stopped for an instant—I knew it had stopped. A gap in time had opened and in that gap only my mind was present. I knew now the world could be halted in its tracks. In my full awareness, my conscious soul could be locked inside one final globule of time, to live out eternity stuck in a single, terminal, thought. I knew I had to find the right thought to keep with me, just in case—one that I would want to think eternally.

The advantage of being a bird was the ability to think, to be rational—to be an *avis sapiens*, as Louis called us.

A breeze was coming up. The quill had drifted east, farther into otter territory, a white speck. Chasing after it could mean another scrape with an otter, this time not so lucky. I shuddered, pulling my feet up tight to my belly. Keep the feet out of the water!

Upon reflection, I imagined how I might swoop down—this time head first, skimming just above the ripples, snatching the quill with my bill, never touching down at all. But an otter might see me coming and, as I passed over, leap up to attack. Most mammals were sly and furtive, their two extra legs a poor trade for a pair of wings, condemning them to scurry and prowl, to slink rather than ascend like birds, with dignity and aplomb. Perhaps in the next life they would be awarded wings—and less grotesque ones than those of their fellow mammals, the bats, a misplaced species which, according to Father, must have returned from the afterlife.

Pragmatically, I concluded that a feather, no matter whose, simply wasn't worth my life. I had barely evaded death only a moment ago and wasn't about to risk it again. "Tempt not the Phoenix," Mother always said. No doubt the otter had deduced from my little sortie that the quill had value. He would shadow it, lurking in underwater shadows, waiting.

But what if one or both of the quills drifted back to Louis's island? Louis might think I had discarded them. He had entrusted me with a mission. Could I let him down?

Yes, I could. I banked hard left and headed for home.

A chronic ditherer, I reconsidered. The purpose of the quills was to help me gain an audience with Cyrus and Alexander. The purpose of meeting with them was to avoid catastrophic war. One quill was already lost—half the opportunity gone. How could I throw away the other half?

Reversing course again, I headed east. The wind was roughing up the lake, small whitecaps goose-pimpling the open water. Procrastination will always make decisions for you—spotting a white feather in white-tipped waves would be impossible. Frankly, it was a relief to let it go.

Troy was awake, he and Father in heated debate—at least Father was.

"And the others?" Father interrogated, his bill stirring up an eddy between them.

Troy's bill was quivering. "I don't know. We separated. I just lost track."

"Lost track!" Father's bill agitated the water, the eddy spinning like a whirlpool. "Leaders don't just lose track of their followers, son—especially a drake. Stiff upper bill!"

Troy tried to give him a defiant stare, but behind it was torment.

"Leaders lead!" Father cried. For emphasis, he froze in his stirring, bubbles and froth stealing away in the dark water. "Why, how do you think I got us where we are today? By letting my family fend for itself?" He asked this in a hoarse whisper, as if it were too self-evident to be worth any more energy. "And your family…"

Anticipating what was coming, Troy interrupted, "Father, don't you dare…"

"Basil?" Mercifully, Mother called out from the nest. She was within earshot of the conversation. "Harold and I are going to round up some slugs for dinner. There's not a thing in the nest and we're absolutely famished. You can ask Marcel and Troy to come along to help, if you'd like—and where is Marcel?"

"And I don't approve of all these fermies I see you ingesting, Troy," Father scolded, somewhat defused, sparing Troy an interrogation about his mate, Belle.

But this reproach seemed to galvanize Troy. "I have been where you have never even dreamed, Father, so don't lecture me. I am two-and-a-half bloody years old. I'll do whatever I please."

Father's plumage puffed like porcupine spines, then he saw me and bit off whatever he was about to utter, but the tension in the water was so thick you could break an egg on it, perish the thought. He gave one last thrash to the water and paddled off in the direction of Mother's voice.

Troy had been gone a year, missing the upheavals on the reserve, but he clearly had endured his own. Compared to his old muscular self, he looked a different drake—almost scrawny. Where he had always been open and bold, he now seemed withdrawn, even a bit devious—and, well, quailed.

"Sorry you had to hear that, Marcel," Troy said. "Father never was very sympathetic—still wants to control everything."

"You didn't happen to see one of my swan pinions floating about, did you, Troy?" I asked, trying to stay out of it.

"Scarce item to be out loose on its own—worth a few acorns, depending on length and condition."

"Troy, what on earth happened to you?" I asked, suddenly feeling very sad for him, knowing he had suffered—was still suffering.

"Harold said he saw you with the pinions at story time, old boy," Troy answered, ignoring my question. "Some sort of talisman, he imagined, knowing your interest in religions and cults and all that. You lost them?"

"It's a long story, the quills—something I would like your advice on, but it can wait. It's your adventure I want to hear, Troy. You've been gone so long. I missed you."

"A dark, dismal tale, brother, utterly depressing—not an adventure at all, unless you consider abject failure an adventure."

The sun had evolved from a hot red ball into a pallid disk that had crept up behind a filmy sheet of cloud edging in from the south, foretelling heavy rain by evening.

"I was proud, Marcel, full of myself," he sighed. "You could see that, couldn't you? To lead a migration, the first duck in our family to leave the reserve, the challenge—how over-confident I was. Being in front, at the point of the V—you can't imagine how much that pumps up the ego. Not one single duck tail in front of you. You think you actually own every pair of wings behind you, to do with as you alone decide."

I could see Father foraging along the bank. Mother must have sent him to search out slugs—what she made him do when he was upset, to calm him.

Troy glanced briefly at Father. "It's all backwards when you start out, you know. You don't feel responsible for them, like you should. You feel they are responsible for you—that they owe you something for being their leader, for having courage."

"You hadn't had that much experience, Troy," I said. "A tenderwebfoot, really. What about Belle?" He had not once mentioned her. They had mated only the day before the migration and I hardly knew her, except that she seemed so practical, in sharp contrast to Troy's daring—complementary traits, I liked to believe. Belle's brother, Nick, had guarded her like a hawk. He didn't seem to like Troy.

Troy began to tremble. "Listen, I picked up some fermies a few hours ago from Jasper's stash. Keeps them in the hollow oak with the Bark."

"Jasper? Our Pastor Jasper?"

"For a preacher, he drives a hard bargain. Want one? I do."

"No thanks, Troy."

"Go ahead, there's some on the bank behind those logs. I've got to pick up the rest later." He nodded toward some beached driftwood. "Father's going to find them in about a minute, if he doesn't change course."

"I just don't have the stomach for fermies."

"I'll need to divert him," Troy said, setting off for the shore with a shout—"Father! I want to apologize!"

As he swam away, I saw Harold in the cove chatting up an attractive younger duck and paddled over to them. The duck looked me up and down.

Excusing my interruption, I asked Harold about Pastor Jasper.

"Says he stocks them only for weddings, right, Francine?" Harold said to his friend, winking at her. "But there's also reported to be some, ah, medicinal usage. Common knowledge, really."

I was born immune to common knowledge.

Troy returned a short while later, exuding the sour reek of moldy apples, a bulge working down his gullet. Father had reversed direction along the bank and was poking about in the long grass. Troy must have reported sighting slugs to him.

"As a rule, I never partake before dark," Troy said with a final gulp and fumy belch, "but Father gets you so riled up, you have to do something."

"You were saying that you were overconfident—as the leader."

"Oh, was I? Well, not that I wouldn't take charge again, little brother. I am cut out for that sort of thing. Made a couple of blunders, all right, but not really my fault—it's the stragglers that foul up your plans, no discipline whatsoever. Sure you won't have a fermie?"

Declining, I made it a point to try to catch Troy in the morning. That would be the time to hear his story, when he was fresh. With pity in my heart, I watched him paddle back toward his cache of apples. Something bad must have happened to him. And there was still the question of what happened to Belle.

Chapter 6

A tranquil rain had drizzled all night, but after my close call with the otter I hardly slept. Troy bobbed a few yards away in a stupor that turned fitful as the night deepened. "Sorghum!" I heard him cry out, and my mind leapt back to the royal funeral and the enigmatic heron who claimed he had come from there. I could still feel the heron's throaty croak rumbling in the water like thunder. A peculiar aura seemed to emanate from him, which at the time I had attributed to the surreal grandeur of the funeral.

On the reserve, events, no matter how shocking, had always remained within the realm of reasonable conceivability, conforming to known physical laws and behavior—a lizard had never popped out of a robin's egg, for example. Whether other laws applied off the reserve was, as far as I could tell, the sort of metaphysical speculation that could never be put to the test—unless one ventured outside to see for oneself, as had Troy, who now floated before me, smelling bad and looking ruined.

"Troy," I asked, "what does Sorghum mean to you?"

The way he recoiled, I thought he'd been struck by an otter. His body convulsed and an unearthly squawk erupted from his gullet.

"Sorghum! What do you know about Sorghum?" he shrieked.

Others stirred awake. Heads slipped out of wings, looking around for the source of the disturbance. A few ducks bolted into a half-launch.

Harold approached, cheerful and sardonic, as always. "It's what you get if you bite a wasp," he laughed. "What's all the fuss?"

"I think Troy had a nightmare," I said.

"I knew that swan pinion would buy him a big hangover," Harold said, shaking his head at Troy, who began to paddle astern.

"Swan pinion?" I quacked. "Hangover?"

"I told him to give it back," Harold said. "But he said, 'Sorry, finders keepers.'"

"Louis Wingstrong gave me that pinion," I said. "In fact, he gave me two. One blew out onto the lake somewhere."

"'Finders keepers,' you said, right, Troy?" Harold shouted at Troy, who had abruptly swum away and launched off the lake.

"Pastor Jasper!" I said. "Troy must have found the pinion and traded it for fermies."

"Marcel, you'd lose your tail if it wasn't stuck on your butt," Harold said.

I made my way through the woods on foot—it was always a trudge, since the brush was too thick to fly through—to the old hollow oak where the Bark was kept. The sun had come out, scattering tufts of light through the grove and gilding the south side of the trunk of the oak, where the hole opened. I couldn't flap up like a cormorant to land on the branch next to the hole—how a webfoot could grip like that was beyond me—but I could hover and briefly peer inside. As I drew up to the hole, flapping hard to maintain equilibrium, the first whiff of fermented fruit almost slammed me to the ground. Recovering, I struggled back up to the hole.

Sure enough, the white sheen of a quill glowed inside.

This was a dilemma. Settling to the ground, I tried to reason.

Inside the tree was Louis' pinion, a ticket of admission to possible peace talks with the warring swan leaders. But, through my neglect, the pinion had found its way into a barter—for an intoxicant! Someone else now had possession—Pastor Jasper. I had to get it back.

On one wing, I could simply reach in and take the feather. But that felt like stealing, even though it belonged to me. Also, I might be seen and reported—even now, a finch was eyeing me from an adjacent birch—and I would have the pastor branding me a criminal to the whole Phoenix congregation.

On the other wing, Pastor Jasper would not be too anxious to stir up a scandal about his fermies trade, or to have to confront Father about Troy's involvement in it. If he found the quill missing, he might keep it to himself. Moreover, I had to keep in mind the ultimate purpose of Louis' gift and ask myself whether the end justified the means—peace on the reserve versus possible impropriety.

The fermie vapor had made me woozy and I was losing my train of thought. Too much dithering—the quill belonged to me, damn it! I rocketed back up to the hole. My head spinning, gagging on the fumes, I darted my bill into the hole, grabbed the feather, dropped to the ground, and scuttled away like a mammal as fast as my webbed feet would take me along the mossy earth, punting aside pine cones, swiped by prickles, wings flailing, the thick canopy of boughs blocking me from a quick aerial escape, my grunting muffled by the quill.

By the time I had made it to the edge of the woods, gasping for breath through clenched bill, my head had cleared and remorse had burrowed into my heart. Through my own carelessness, I had lost both quills. I had only myself to blame. The object I gripped tightly in my bill no longer belonged to me—at least as I understood the law of ownership. After all, didn't the Sixth Presentment clearly state it? *Claim what you can prevent others from claiming.* The quill had to be returned. It was self-delusion to think I could steal for a higher purpose. Idealism was for birds who could dream great dreams and step on their better natures. Unfortunately, I wasn't one of those.

I pivoted and trudged back toward the hollow oak. The finch had departed. Through the fluttering leaves, I could see a wink of red. On the branch next to the hole perched Pastor Jasper. I felt a deep gnaw in the pit of my gizzard.

"And what have you got there, pinched so tightly in your bill, Marcel, my boy?" Pastor Jasper inquired in his droll, affected Cardinalese accent, his head feathers stiffly erect in practiced simulation of a crest. "Why, a fine, snowy-white, swan quill, it appears," he observed, answering his own question, and as if shocked by the discovery, "whole and intact, most likely a trumpeter pinion, by the length of it, scarce as hens' teeth, they are."

"It's not what you think, Pastor Jasper," I said, the cloying odor of fermies from the oak flooding over me. I realized that the Stump and Bark had always reeked of fermies. Perhaps I had dismissed it as some kind of holy fragrance.

"Might it be that you're taking it for a little stroll, then?" he said. "Just out on a bit of a lark?"

"It didn't belong to Troy," I said, looking up at him, dropping the feather in front of me. "But you can have it back."

He hopped nervously from foot to foot on his perch. "And what does your good brother have to do with this?"

"You'll have to put it back in the tree yourself, though. I can't take the fermie fumes."

"The fermies, ah, yes," he exclaimed in a higher pitch, dancing more energetically, "excellent preservative for the Bark. Might have rotted long ago but for the alcohol, praise Phoenix."

"The quill was given to me by Louis."

"Louis, poor devil," Pastor Jasper commiserated, one eye squinting. "Won't be needing them, will he, except to keep the chill off. I wonder how many more he'd be willing to part with, assuming a mild winter, of course."

"He gave me two, actually, and I lost them both."

"Two, did he, now."

"They were supposed to be peace offerings for Cyrus and Alexander."

"A certain nihilistic resignation, to be discarding one's equipment like that—sad, especially for a king, but an opportunity, happily, for the lad to perhaps find the Phoenix and save his soul, before it's too late. It's never too late to experience the Response, you know," he said, the opposite eye now squinting and the other opening wide as he seemed to ponder a new thought. "What about Alexander? A swan more interested in political power than his proclaimed service to the Phoenix, dare I speak behind his tail, but he gives me a devil of a time, truth be told, a real beakful of bother."

"Louis thought a quill each for Cyrus and Alexander might bring them together for talks—they still respect the Wingstrongs."

"Respect! Cyrus? This heathen cannot respect—nor be respected!" Unable to confine himself to his perch, Pastor Jasper leapt up, fluttered in an excited circle, wings blurred and whapping. Coming to rest on the rim of the hole, he inhaled deeply, his crest twitching like a little blood-red tongue. "You cannot trust him, especially with anything so valuable. No telling what mischief would result from putting a trumpeter quill in his greedy beak." Inhaling again, he puffed up his feathers, which then flattened in contentment as the fermies took effect. "Not that that rascal Alexander is any better, may Phoenix forgive me—he is brethren, after all. Where did you say the other quill was?"

"How much do you want for this one, Pastor Jasper?" I picked up Louis' pinion, feeling its shaft and silky fringe in my bill.

"Want for it?" Through the black sapsucker mask, both his eyes squinted down at me, flicking back and forth as if counting thoughts. "Why, I'd want you to just have it, my boy, but I couldn't just give it to you, could I? I mean the uncompensated reduction in inventory I would suffer—of the produce, that is, that your good brother purchased. But your father and I have been friends for so long, partners in the faith…" He trailed off, peering into the distance. "Ah!" he suddenly chirped. "A fine trumpeter pinion such as this is worth at least a thousand acorns on the open market—you must know that." His voice dropped to a conspiratorial whisper. "I'll let you have it for two hundred—no, one hundred acorns. But, of course, not a word to your father—he'd question my sanity, letting it go for that."

The accumulation of acorn wealth was seasonal and autumn was still a month away. With competition from squirrels and other birds, it would take me that plus another month to find and gather a hundred acorns—not to mention the difficulty of safekeeping a stockpile. The traditional method of reserve banking—digging a hole in the bank of the lake—had not proved very secure. In any case, the swans would be past the point of compromise by then. I would have to approach them without quills to offer, empty-billed. Feeling too deflated even to fly, I left the woods and plodded back to the marsh.

"All right, ninety acorns!" Pastor Jasper called out behind me. "But have them by Wednesday."

Ninety, a hundred, it made no difference. I would ask Troy to negotiate.

Chapter 7

Silhouettes of pines stood against a sky the color of purple asters. A fat moon had risen to the east, inviting all to approach on the silver flecks it had strewn across the lake. I had never looked forward more to one of Mother's soothing recitals—just to float, to listen, to lose myself in a story.

"Marcel!" It was Father's voice, echoing across the dark water.

"I'm here, Father," I called back.

"Troy's gone missing," he shouted. He came up paddling hard, his bill thrashing the water.

I told myself I couldn't deal with another calamity today.

"Quills!" Father squawked. "What do you know about some trumpeter quills?" He floated before me, alarm in his eyes.

I had never seen Father so disturbed. He must have found out from Harold about Troy and the fermies and confronted him, Troy running off in anger, shame and guilt. My peace mission to the swans had turned into a confused family mess. No matter how altruistic the original prize, all efforts eventually seem to gravitate towards the valuables—the quills, in this case.

"Louis gave me two pinions, Father," I said. "I lost them when Troy came home. One drifted out on the lake. I searched for hours but couldn't find it."

Father was still trying to catch his breath. "Well, Harold said Troy went on some damned fool hunt for it over on the east side of the marsh. Should have been back two hours ago."

The east side was otter territory.

"This is my fault," I said to Father.

"Doesn't matter whose fault. Main thing is to find Troy. Your mother and I have already lost too many of your brothers and sisters, son," Father said, sending my heart into a plunge. "Not to mention the ones we lost in the broods before yours."

The plan was for Harold and me to comb the eastern shoreline at low altitude, while Father, Uncle Arthur and five cousins zigzagged the open lake, all of us calling out to Troy.

Mother tried to hide her worry. "Eat something," she insisted to Father. "None of you will be any use without energy." You could sense her foreboding—Basil Jr., Phoebe, Irene, and now Troy.

By the time we launched from the lake, night had fallen. Duck vision is sharp in moonlight, but flying so low along the shore, we risked smashing into overhanging tree limbs. Harold took the lead, always valiant when the chicks were down. I flew just behind, off his starboard wing, weaving with him as he swerved to avoid branches, shouting, "Bogey ahead!" to me each time. All the while we cried out to Troy, hearing, like an echo, the distant chant of his name from Father's group farther out above the lake.

Up and down along the banks we flew, pass after pass—nothing, only the feeble clatter of frogs and crickets and the eerie hoot of an owl.

As we flew, I had time to consider the dreadful chain of events the quills had triggered—that I had triggered. As if reading my mind, Harold glanced back at me.

"What you were doing with those pinions, anyway, Marcel?" he asked, veering sharply to miss a willow. "Yikes, almost hit that one."

"A mistake, just a big mistake, Harold," I said. And, in the back of my mind, I knew that there was much more grief to come.

The moon had risen higher, pouring cold light upon the black marsh, making it glisten.

"Look!" Harold shouted.

He pitched down abruptly. I followed in a steep dive. A white quill was bobbing just off a rocky point. Harold scooped it up in his bill and shot upwards, climbing with powerful wing strokes.

"Blood," he said, as we leveled off. "I taste blood."

We went to fetch the others. Our search would now be driven more by weary resolve than hope. My heart was so weighted it seemed to push down into my gizzard. Our flapping settled into a doleful rhythm. Our calls to Troy all but petered out. The moon had arced to the west and an amber glow was tinting the eastern horizon when Father called it off.

"We've got to take care of ourselves, now," he said, wheeling slowly around toward home. "Cousins up front."

The five cousins assembled into a small V. Uncle Arthur drew up abeam of Father, who lagged aft. Behind them, Harold and I brought up the rear. "I'm sorry, Basil." Uncle Arthur said.

"All for a bloody swan feather. I don't know what to say to Doris, Arthur."

"You know, Marcel," Harold said to me, "now that I think about it, this quill tastes more like fish than blood."

At that moment, I heard duck wings coming up hard from behind.

"Marcel, Harold," Troy's voice panted.

I felt the same sublime relief as when I had escaped the otter's teeth.

Chapter 8

"A wild goose chase! Another of his larks!" Father barked, spinning his bill into the lake like a waterspout. But Mother nestled up close, trying to console him.

"We have Troy back, Basil—what more could we ask?" she soothed.

"He's not the same drake! He's not the son who led a great migration!" Father railed, plunging his head into the water. He came up sputtering, "We're all disgraced, Doris."

Indeed, it was clear that something had happened to change my brother. I had not been able to find out what it was—and maybe never would, considering how well he kept his distance. Ducks seem unusually prone to fermie craving, our sparse taste buds oddly tuned to royal tastes—escargot, slugs and fermented fruit. I have known a few cousins whose lives were ruined by their careless appetites—"otter fodder," Uncle Arthur called them.

I ached for Troy to return to his old self—how endearingly cocky he used to be—and I longed to know what misfortune he had met on his migration, what had so tortured him, driven him to fermies, and what connection there was to Sorghum. But he refused to talk and you can't get blood from a stone. Mother said we birds never tire of trying to get the response we want from each other. Louis said there would always be work for priests because we are ceaselessly trying to get the entire universe to do what we want. I guess there is always something outside our control.

Harold, honorable as always, returned the found quill to me—or maybe he brought back a curse. Now, I would have to pursue talks with the swans. At least the other quill was reasonably safe with Jasper until I could redeem it.

With only one quill left, I wondered which to approach, the mutes or the tundras. Ignoring the concerned voice in my head that advised neither, it seemed most logical and safe to start with Alexander, chief of the mutes. The mutes worshipped the Phoenix. I reasoned that Alexander would be more sympathetic to someone from my family—members of his own faith. Cyrus, naturally, would immediately be suspicious of any bird not a Horus.

Conversely, a duck who was able to gain a peace overture from Cyrus and the tundras might impress Alexander and convince him to come to the peace table on behalf of the mutes—but that was a long shot. No, the mutes were a better bet—right off the bats, as they say.

Of course, I couldn't overlook the fact that Alexander and Cyrus were both cagey bargainers—either one might take the quill just for openers and expect more after that. I didn't want to end up throwing good pinions after bad, not that I could even ask Louis to contribute more, especially with winter coming on.

I decided to consult Father.

"Absolutely not," Father said point-blank. "Too dangerous, even the mutes—and I already told you how much I distrust the tundras."

"Louis was in favor," I protested with a timid whine in my quack, the best way to cement Father's opinion—I hoped he would talk me out of the whole idea. "He gave me the quills."

"Louis! Sending a duckling on a drake's mission, the coward! Why, you're afraid of your own shadow—not that you can help it, son, it's in your nature, you were born nervous."

Happily, I couldn't dispute that. "So you think I should forget about all this, Father?" I hinted.

He bit back his answer. A light grew in his eyes. He took a drink from the lake and released a good-natured belch. "Forget about it? Why, you don't have to do a thing, Marcel."

Freed! My fears departed in a rush like a flock of starlings from a cottonwood. A great load seemed to fall from my wings. My gut untightened. I felt light-headed—seaweed waved dizzily in the murky shallows under my feet.

Father cleared his gullet. "Not on your own, anyway," he declared. "I'm going with you—I mean, you're coming with me."

Chapter 9

All my anxiety came rushing back like flies to a beached carp.

I had never seen Father so charged with vitality. "Don't you see, son?" he rhapsodized, "this could be an historic opportunity. An old drake like me wants to leave a legacy, you know—to contribute to the community and to have his contribution recognized, honored."

"A legacy?"

"Something to be remembered for, son—not for me, of course, for your Mother, mainly, and our broods, to be proud of. Frankly, this thing with Troy has besmirched the family name a bit."

"We're all proud of you already, Father."

"I can picture it," he swelled. "Cyrus will respect me, a sincere elder, despite that he's a Horus, Phoenix save his soul. I'll convince him how the Phoenix stands for unity. He'll see that. And once I soften up Cyrus and have his trust, Alexander will buy in." He closed his eyes, inviting his vision of a truce, a truce arranged by him. "Now," he commanded, eyes snapping open, "bring me that quill, son. And tell Troy to freshen up. He'll have a chance to redeem himself on this mission. Maybe Harold should come, too. He could learn something about responsibility. Oh, and don't say anything to your mother. She's a worrier, like you."

It's amazing how the voice of confidence can drag you forward when your instincts shout "No!" Even when you know better, even when you have the power to stand against, to resist—somehow, the will submits. I deferred to Father because I had always believed he had the best interests of our family at heart, because I respected him, because I was used to granting him authority, and, with all his broods, he was used to taking it—and also because he did issue orders so confidently, as if he had already considered all possible consequences. His demeanor directed that what we were asked was a patriotic duty, beyond question.

In any case, it was a relief to turn the quill over to Father.

He set a time two days ahead for a meeting with the tundras, bribing a young Canada goose with the promise of half a dozen slugs to carry the message to Cyrus and sending me out to find the slugs.

Harold was dubious. "If I were Cyrus and a duck brought me a trumpeter pinion, I would take the pinion—for starters. Then I would up the ante. We ought to take him a few acorns and save the pinion for the grand finale. Let him earn it."

Troy wanted to bring fermies—to ease the tension, he argued. He had agreed to come along—after some insensitive but persuasive shaming by Father. "Do you want to be forever remembered as the Bloedel drake who lost an entire flock, Troy? And brought disgrace to his family?"

"What's our strategy?" Harold asked Father when we met on the west shore the afternoon before the day of our mission.

Father gave him a dismissive snort. "Strategy? Why, the Phoenix will guide us, Harold—with a divine strategy. This will be a blessed mission, son. We must put aside our mortal pretensions. Cyrus will greet me as an agent of the Creator." He looked up at the sky, haphazard with small clouds. "We are called."

We all looked up, the stiff breeze ruffling our back feathers. One cloud sped across the sun, extinguishing the happy glint of the lake.

"What about Odetta?" Harold asked.

I had almost forgotten that she now lived with the tundras.

"Well, what about her?" Father replied, his foot on the quill to keep it from blowing away.

He had lain the quill on the grass between us. He carried it with him everywhere, sleeping with it clenched in his bill, as I had, despite Mother's gentle sarcasm—"Is it your turn, dear, or Marcel's? I can never remember whose night it is to sleep with the feather."

Harold glanced at the quill. "What will she think when we give Cyrus one of Louis' pinions?" he inquired.

For a brief moment, Father looked perplexed, then he fluffed himself together, the set of his bill resolute. "Not a factor, Harold. Don't confuse the issue. This is serious business, drake business."

We set off at daybreak—Father in front, with the pinion, Troy, Harold and me astern—swimming across the cove to the bank, which formed one boundary of the plush lawn the tundras had taken from the mutes. The honks of the swans were faint, but, to me, already ominous.

"Let's hope that goose told them we were coming," Harold said.

Once we had climbed ashore, the honking grew louder, and sounded fiercer. I plucked two fat slugs from a dew-wetted stone. Food was always a comfort. We had left before breakfast in order not to wake Mother, but she had called out as we swam off, "Basil, you know how touchy Cyrus can be. Don't say anything you'll regret."

This had stirred Madeline out of her sleep. "You'll be careful, Marcel, won't you?" Actually, it's impossible to be careful when someone else is in charge.

Along the bank, beneath a cottonwood, there was a stand of tall grasses and Queen Anne's lace, and through it we could see white patches moving.

"Bogeys ahead," Harold said.

I felt my flesh tingle. My stomach began to gurgle. I should have passed up the slugs, which digest best late in the day, or at least when the nerves are calm.

We emerged from the undergrowth, stepping onto a spongy, lush lawn. The mansion rose at the far edge, its broad white elevation tinted pink in the glare of the rising sun, the reflection of which in an upper window blinded me for an instant, so that I almost walked into a swan—one of six that barred our way.

"Good, our greeting party," Father said to them. "Tell Cyrus that Basil is here to see him."

"They're either stupid or suicidal," one of the swans said.

"He's got a trumpeter quill, like Cyrus said, Colonel," another pointed out.

"Take it," the first one said, apparently the leader.

Father fixed him with a hard stare. "This is for Cyrus only."

My gizzard issued a distress call that I was sure could be heard across the reserve.

"Father…" Harold said.

The colonel gave Father an amused look. "All right, let him have his moment of glory," he laughed.

Flanked by our escorts, we trudged across the lawn toward a dense concentration of swans. As we drew close, I could see that they were aligned into columns of about fifty swans each, every swan propped on one leg, all together like an orchard of white-blossoming saplings—conformity being the common denominator of militant societies, according to Mother. "You can't love your neighbor and play soldier at the same time, dear," she said when Father once wanted to organize a duck defense league, "or have fun."

Perhaps inspired by the regimentation, Father set a bracing pace. "Get in step," he ordered. "Left, right, left, right…" Our escorts, disciplined, complied unconsciously, and Troy also fell in, but Harold and I stumbled and almost fell, having no sense of it at all.

At the head of the swans stood Cyrus, more compact than I remembered since my last sight of him at Edward's funeral—or maybe he just seemed smaller compared to Odetta, who, reposing on one leg at his side, dwarfed all the tundras. As we approached, Cyrus spread his wings and stood up on his toes for effect. Nevertheless, his head barely reached Odetta's shoulder.

Our party halted before the tundra chief. At close range, any swan can look enormous and threatening to a duck. Cyrus, and the corpus of hostile energy issuing from the tundra formation behind him, made my legs weak. I looked at Troy, whose feathers were visibly trembling.

"Sir," Father declared, apparently not intimidated, "I am Basil, elder mallard of the west cove. On behalf of all concerned citizens of Bloedel Reserve, I bring you this peace offering." He laid the trumpeter quill on the cushiony, spring-green turf, which, underfoot, felt comforting but oddly out of place, being in such stark contrast to the hard ranks of soldiers camped upon it—a captured luxury, not an earned one, although I suppose some do not make a distinction between taking and earning.

Silence ensued, as fraught with menace as the instant before an earthquake, when the entire reserve senses it coming, not yet knowing the severity.

At that moment, four swans sailed overhead—mutes, probably, because they were bigger than the tundras and the latter, like good soldiers, all seemed to be present and accounted for on the lawn.

"A peace offering," Father repeated, a slightly more expectant, but not servile, tone in his voice.

"Father," Harold whispered, "he heard you—lower your eyes."

"A peace offering," Cyrus mimicked in a falsetto quack to no one in particular. "The little duck has a peace offering."

The colonel sniggered. This was the cue for the rest of the tundras, who broke into boisterous guffaws.

"Silence!" Cyrus honked.

The uproar ceased as if shoved underwater.

Odetta's gaze shifted to the quill. "That's a trumpeter pinion, Cy," she said.

Her mere stature demanded attention. She was a gorgeous bird—so tall, sleek and muscular that you couldn't take your eyes off her.

"Where did you find this?" Cyrus said.

"I feel like I've been violated, Cy," Odetta said. "You know, seeing it there, lying on the ground, out in the open and all."

"Let me handle this, Odetta," Cyrus said.

A long, low blare issued from Odetta's beak, rising to a harsh, menacing riff, like a call to arms. Her head swiveled back to survey the ranks. The army of tundras stirred.

Danger crawled over my skin. Harold and I exchanged glances. "Control issues," he whispered. If it weren't for Father, we would both have launched at that instant and fled for our lives. But we couldn't leave him—or Troy, who was in a weakened state.

Father opened his wings and reared up. "A gift, Cyrus, to you," he quacked, "donated by our, ah, retired king, Louis Wingstrong, to foster peace on the reserve—peace, between the followers of the Phoenix, may he bless us all, and those of the Horus persuasion, may we all find unity in truth."

Odetta's head snapped forward at the mention of Louis.

"Father—get down!" Harold pleaded in a whisper.

Father settled down, casting a squat shadow on the grass. Finally, he lowered his eyes. "I, sir, am only the messenger, of course."

"He talks like that pipsqueak sapsucker that's always spoutin' off," one of the guards said.

"Louis?" Odetta hissed. "That quill came from Louis?"

"Yes, ma'am," Father beamed. "Must have caused him no small measure of pain to pull out."

Odetta advanced on Father so suddenly and with such fury that I thought she would chop him dead on the spot. Cyrus hopped between them just in time but was sent sprawling on top of Father.

"The spineless lout!" Odetta exploded. "I'll tear out his heart if I ever see him again."

"Flock!" honked the colonel. Instantly, the motionless army of swans dropped all feet to the ground and began to agitate and growl.

"Let's get out of here," Harold quacked, barging under Cyrus' wing to shove Father free.

I didn't have to be told twice. I took one deep breath and launched, glancing back to see Troy coming up behind and Father and Harold, just airborne, leaving their shadows on the ground. Luckily, none of the swans took off in pursuit—no reason to, I suppose. We hadn't done any harm and Cyrus now owned the quill—or Odetta, whoever was in charge.

We formed up, with Harold taking the point. "Tough crowd," he said.

"She didn't give me a chance," Father wheezed, flapping hard. "I had him right where I wanted him."

"The best laid plans of grouse and hen," Harold said, "oft go awry, Father. We're lucky to have escaped with our lives."

We were north of the mansion. Ahead lay the rough green clearing where the tundras had ousted the mutes—only temporary refugees, Alexander had pledged, until they could reclaim the lawn.

Harold began a rounded turn south, back to our cove.

I felt it coming more than saw it and banked hard to starboard. A white mass shot by, just missing me—swhoosh!

"Bogeys!" Harold called, rolling out into a steep, inverted dive, Troy splitting off to the left, Father making a lumbering turn right. Two white shapes rocketed down between them.

Evidently, I was wrong about the tundras—they weren't done with us. We formed up again, covering Harold's flank.

Behind me, I heard a thump as something hit Father. He squawked, tumbled out of formation and spun earthward, wings akimbo.

"They're mutes!" Troy called out, trying to sweep under Father and break his fall—but he was too late.

As Father plummeted down, the sound of his quacks fading, I heard a vicious hiss.

"Traitors!" It was Alexander's voice. "We saw you consorting with the enemy! You will all pay!" But the mutes broke off as Harold came at them—deft in the air, his valor more than offset any disadvantage in size.

Father was unconscious. He had struck a tall evergreen on the way down, and this had broken his fall, but the impact of the swan must have injured him badly. He lay on a pad of brown pine needles, eyes closed, panting, one wing at an odd angle, a sporadic twitch rippling along his feathers.

Harold sent Troy to fetch Mother, then turned to me. "We need to get him to a nest, Marcel," he said, but that, of course, was impossible.

"Can't we make one?" I suggested. Any action was better than standing there.

We raked up some pine needles and banked them up around Father. Harold added a couple of small, dried branches and some ferns. I worked in a few pine cones to the improvised structure, which looked pitifully lacking for an injured father.

It seemed inconceivable for Father to be unconscious. I didn't recall his ever being wounded or ill. The sight of his limp form was so shocking that I couldn't think—for the first time in my life, I couldn't think. A wave of grief passed through me. It took all my strength to keep from slipping my head under a wing, to blot out the sight of him lying there, helpless, and the sound of his too-quick breathing.

In a matter of minutes, Mother glided in to land a step away from Father, her wings arching over him. Without a word, she rested her head on the back of his neck, listening, feeling, transmitting. Harold, Troy and I stood back, praying for something to do, some way to help.

For over an hour, Mother lay beside Father, her wings nesting him.

Abruptly, his eyes opened. "Doris," he groaned.

My heart leapt. Troy and I rushed forward together, quacking, but Harold stopped us. "Shush...let him breathe, let him talk."

"Doris," Father said, choking a bit, "I'm dying." A pink froth bubbled from his beak.

"Nonsense, Basil," Mother said, "you just had a nasty fall." But her voice was full of sorrow.

"You must do something for me, Doris, you must do it now, while there's time," Father said.

"There's all the time in the world, dear," she said.

That is when I first comprehended that there isn't all the time in the world.

"Listen," Father said, his eyes dull. "I want you to remove this tag on my leg. I can't bloody die banded like this. Do that for me, Doris."

Mother raised her head, her eyes searching first Harold's, then Troy's, then mine—an agonized look.

Harold moved closer. "Father, it's Harold. The band is metal."

"I'm not bloody stupid, Harold," Father said, lifting his head, an enormous effort. "If it was simple, I would have done it already. But eventually we're all going to die, aren't we? You have to plan ahead. I can't meet the Phoenix banded by the likes of Clout, can I?" His head fell back.

"Tell me what you want me to do, Father, and I will do it," Harold said, glancing at Mother. "We will do it."

"Swear to me, son."

"With my foot on the Bark, Father."

Father sighed. "Then bring a hawk. Tell him to bite off my leg."

Mother jumped. "No!"

"Father, you can't!" Harold cried, trapped by his oath, his wings beating, stirring a flurry of pine needles into the air.

"But—hawks pray to Horus, Father," I tried, desperate, holding back sobs.

"Then he'll enjoy it all the more. Tell him he can have the rest of me after I'm gone. Carrion, I know, but fresh and healthy. I've thought this all out. And no jays at the funeral."

Chapter 10

"Family and friends of the deceased," Pastor Jasper began, perched on his customary pulpit limb midway up the maple, opposite the sacred oak, from which fermie fumes—I was acutely conscious of them now—wafted through the grove, where we were assembled for Father's funeral, "we gather here to honor our dearly departed Basil, a mallard who has, so sadly for us— so doubly sad, insofar as we were unable to arrange a viewing…"

At this, Mother let out a wail. Before performing the leg amputation, the hawk had abruptly severed Father's neck. "As a raptor, I can't stand to see a bird suffer," she said, while we gaped in stunned disbelief. "I'm sorry, but professional decisions have to be made—above the interests of any one individual."

"…who has, I say," Pastor Jasper resumed after a respectful pause, "passed over to a better place—where, of course, we all eventually must follow—to be freed of our earthly trials, released from our sins, unchained from our fears."

Here, he rested a beat, his feigned cardinal crest erect, head tilted, black eyes shining down at us. It had only been a day since Father's death. Our parish, absent the mutes, gazed back with the numbness of survivors—glad, as was I, it seemed, for refuge in the ritual of a funeral. Only Troy had reacted vengefully—trying to plot retaliation, demanding compensation. Uncle Arthur had had to calm him down. "One funeral is enough, Troy," he said.

"But…" Pastor Jasper went on, his voice ringing out in a higher register, "as the Second Presentment commands us—*Never, never cease to bargain with the Creator for pardon!*"

"Tell it, Jasper!" Jerome whistled, more to call attention to himself than to spur on the eulogy. He had shown up uninvited. If nothing else, jays are brazen. He pecked at a chestnut taken from the pile of hors d'oeuvres, meant for later.

"We know, my dear ones," Pastor Jasper continued, with an appreciative nod to Jerome, "that in this troubled life on earth, all fear can be overcome—nay, conquered!—even the fear, dare I utter it before you, of death."

Taking a breath, he sent a blink of consolation to Mother.

"'The fear of death conquered,' you wonder, 'how is that possible?'" he went on, not waiting for a reply. "And I answer, 'By submitting to the Phoenix.' We—all who serve him—must obey his commands, must act according to the Presentments, must choose to make hard sacrifices in his name. Only then will the Phoenix, in his great mercy, lead us to that yearned-for path, a long, rich life on earth, an extended life, my beloveds!—not everlasting, of course, but perhaps significantly, ah, prolonged. And finally, he will grant us our place in heaven, with all its magnificence and glory—not the least of which, I'm certain, will be freedom from our burden of wings, since there will be no predators to flee in Paradise."

Since we have never received a report of actual conditions in heaven, I suppose it is each bird's privilege to tweak his or her view of the situation there, but I wondered if Pastor Jasper had consulted with Louis before canonizing this theory. Frankly, I couldn't imagine the Creator would have bestowed the power of wings upon us, only to snatch it away, leaving only the yearning for flight. This was something humans did.

I scanned the grove, downhearted not to see Louis, or at least his sister, Melody, who, having nested alone on the north shore since her parents died, still ought to have known about

Father. There were, in fact, no swans at all in attendance. The tundras would not, for any reason, associate with followers of the Phoenix, and the presence of a single mute—anger at these murderers was stirring under my grief—would have tainted the ceremony. Yet I knew that Alexander, in his boundless arrogance, bullied his way into every Phoenix assembly, and I had been dreading the sight of his long, white neck and masked head among the mourners.

I must concede that I couldn't help looking around at the mourners—to be distracted, perhaps, from my own morbid introspection, or to feel enfolded in communal sorrow and less isolated in my own; or, and may Phoenix forgive me, because in the aftermath of death, any sign of life, any vitality, is almost thrilling.

I was sitting close to Mother, to her right, at the edge of the grove, bordering a patch of ferns and fallen leaves. Harold sat to Mother's left, Troy and Madeline behind, the four of us a tight fortress around her, sending her swells of solace, but to no avail—her ceaseless weeping punctuated by shudders and deep, mournful quacks, which would provoke wails of lamentation from other birds, especially the more emotional doves.

At the rear of the grove I was startled to recognize the same green heron that had come from Sorghum to attend Edward's funeral. Thinking of Troy's reaction to my mention of Sorghum, I glanced at my brother, but he seemed not to have noticed the mysterious stranger. I looked back at the heron, catching in his sinuous poise a fleeting sense of his fine savagery, reaching back to the most ancient bloodlines.

Hearing a rustle, I peered into the ferns and saw that a small garter snake was shedding its skin. The old, dry tube, a dull, dead husk, was peeling back. The snake, its new skin alive with an oily, greenish black shine, was writhing forward, struggling to be free of the clinging membrane. Its eyes were milked over—protected from the ordeal, but temporarily blinded. It reminded me of my molt, when feathered anew, I realized that underneath I was still Marcel, the same timid drake.

Pastor Jasper had paused for effect and was now pointing a crimson wingtip at us. "My suffering friends, how many fears do you crave to be freed from?" Having been invited to attempt this sum at every funeral for years, we of course knew the obligatory answer but had perfected an eager-to-be-enlightened silence. Pastor Jasper surveyed each muzzled beak and bill. "More than you have feathers, I would reckon," came the familiar homily.

He paused again. "But there is only one true fear, my friends, the fear of death."

I always dreaded this part of the sermon because I knew he was right. I did have more fears than feathers, and I was terrified of dying."

Yet, in the two days since Father's passing, my comprehension of fear had changed. I suddenly understood that, while there might be dozens of varieties of fear, there were only two modes of death—death with and without dignity.

Father had shown me that. Knowing this new fact somehow reduced my myriad fears down to one—not the fear of death, per se, but of a cowardly death. And, hazily forming in my mind, was the notion that a cowardly death would most likely result from a cowardly life.

Across the grove, there was a disturbance as some late visitors arrived. Peering over Mother's back, I saw Alexander and three mute swans pushing and swaggering their way toward us through a section of ducks.

The ducks were squawking in protest, a few braver ones flapping up with their heads thrust forward in vituperation, but in a moment, Alexander stood towering above Mother, casting her in shadow.

"My deepest sympathy, Doris," he swelled, his bulging white breast like the crown of some giant fungus. "A tragedy—terrible misunderstanding, my dear. If there is anything I can do, you must not hesitate to ask."

Mother, barely aware of his presence, lost in her grief, gave him a dazed stare. I felt her heart searching elsewhere—beyond the sky, the lake, the mountains, beyond existence.

"Leave her alone and get out of here," Troy said. His voice was hard, and as valiant as that morning long ago when he had departed to lead the migration. He hadn't tasted a fermie since Father was killed—he quit cold turkey—and I had wondered how the smell of fermentation from the oak was affecting him.

Alexander leveled a look of irked amusement at my brother. "I'm sure you're upset about your daddy, little duck, so I'm going to overlook your show of disrespect—this time."

My stomach lurched as Troy began to shift his weight from foot to foot, his wings flexing and clamping.

"Troy," Harold said.

Hearing another whisper in the leaves, I saw that the snake had wriggled free of its skin and was slithering off—just as, with a screeching quack, Troy launched from his flatfooted stance, nearly bowling over Mother. He plowed straight into Alexander, wings flailing, his bill punching wildly at the swan's neck.

Stunned for an instant, dodging Troy's thrusts by instinct, Alexander recovered and swatted him aside with a powerful sweep of his wing. Troy tumbled tail over bill past Alexander's henchmen, spinning to a stop, his back against the sacred oak. Alexander let out a guffaw, loud for a mute swan. "Little quacker's got gumption," he honked, "but mute trumps duck."

Something came over me. I felt my muscles tense and my quills tighten against my skin. Blood pounded in my ears. My bowels emptied. Leaping up, I lunged at Alexander, nipping at the stringy black stalks of his legs. I managed to clamp my bill on a leg and bit down for all I was worth, wishing grimly that the Creator had equipped ducks with a real set of teeth.

Teeth or not, once you have dedicated yourself to that task and to that alone, holding on to something with your bill can be an extremely rapt affair. Above me, I heard Alexander squeal. I hung on, his berserk kicks whipping me left and right, scuffing my underside across sharp stones, my neck snapping back and forth.

"Marcel! Stop!" I heard a duck screech. It was Madeline. The sound of her voice broke my concentration, and a glimpse of her rushing into the fray damped my fire.

My grip loosened. Alexander's next kick flung me a good three wingspans, straight into Troy, who was steaming towards us, having bounced back from his crash into the oak. "Harold! Get Mother out of here!" Troy squawked.

I flipped upright in time to see Harold herding Mother from behind, steering her in the direction of the path to the lake and out of the woods, where they could launch. At the same time, two of Alexander's gang, ramrod-straight necks stretched low to the ground, orange beaks scissoring, eyes blazing through their black masks, were charging at Madeline, who had shuffled, flustered and dumbstruck, nearly under Alexander's feet. "Madeline, run!" I quacked.

Too late—the mutes reared up and hacked their beaks down upon Madeline's frail back with terrific chops. She jumped up, then went down, limp, her wings sprawled out upon the debris of feathers and leaves.

I gasped in horror. Once more, the universe slowed, as if the river of time had abruptly tipped uphill, the many tributaries and rivulets of fate drawn to a crawl by a freakish gravity. There were the brute white bulks of the swans, fanning wings in slow motion—Alexander, almost frozen, ponderous, up on his toes, wings unfurled—Harold and Mother, barely moving, too sluggish in their escape—and Madeline, my Madeline, who at that precise moment had entrapped the whole world—Madeline, whose agony was bringing it all to a stop.

My eyes went out of focus. The blurred images of the swans swayed before me, then seemed to replicate—two more

80   *Donald J. Berk*

massive, snowy figures materialized in my vision, one on the ground, the other sailing just above.

A piercing blast rang through the clearing—Louis!—followed by another peal, which took me an instant to recognize—Melody!

A ferocious honking and thrashing of wings erupted. Thick, alabaster snakes with black-and-orange-tipped heads coiled back and struck at each other, and black, webbed hooves stamped the stony ground, kicking up pebbles, feathers, sticks and bits of leaf, which rained upon Madeline, silent and motionless in the midst of the fury.

I made my way toward her, the fight raging on every side, bony, sinewy wings sweeping in to club me, all the while the smells of blood, hate and fermentation surging in my nostrils.

Reaching Madeline, I stretched my wings to shelter her — just as one of the mutes, Melody in pursuit, launched into the dense tree canopy, lost its momentum and plummeted down on top of us.

I awoke to the most beautiful harmony I had ever heard—sweet, sad, delicate, perishable, yet with a web of energy that seemed to quake the core of my being, radiating light to the most distant corners of the universe. Every phrase and trill drew from me a climactic emotion, from joy to aching melancholy. The music dissolved every impulse of worry and regret. I imagined, in a vision of my final moment of consciousness, balanced on the cusp between life and death, where I would be frozen for all eternity, how I would want to be left with only this song, that it was the alchemy of creation itself, preserved.

And then I also knew that something had reached Louis's heart, because it was he, he and Melody, who were playing this music, the sweetest song I'd ever heard.

Chapter 11

Thanks to me, Madeline and Father were dead. It was I who lured them to their ends. It was no one else's fault—not the tundras' or the mutes'—only mine.

I had killed Father with my dreamy, ignorant selfishness. My purported altruistic search for peace on the reserve was entirely in my own interests. I had known nothing about the world, nothing about power, diplomacy, barter and, especially, the shrewd use of wealth—how, once put into play, valuable items like trumpeter pinions gravitate directly to those who crave them. Anyone could have predicted the consequences of my reckless incompetence.

As for my attack on Alexander, what it led to...words fail me.

My bungling had killed two so dear to me and it was more than I could bear. I expected to be punished—deserved it, prayed for it, willed it. It would be divine justice, and the sooner the better. Didn't the Third Presentment tell us, *Error hatches death*? If anyone deserved to die, it was I, the very author of death.

But nothing happened. I was not even treated as an outcast. Instead, after Madeline's brief funeral—for those who had not already fled the grove, a short lamentation by Pastor Jasper tacked onto Father's rites—I received outpourings of condolence. "Poor Marcel," Aunt Olive comforted me, "I don't see how you can stand it—and with not a single offspring, my dear." I even received sympathy for the numerous scrapes inflicted on my underside by Alexander, even though they had long ago scarred over, sending out only an occasional twinge of pain to remind me of the fight.

Sympathy had the effect of making my suffering feel even more illegitimate. In my guilt, I staved off my impulse to visit Louis to thank him. You cannot thank someone whose trust you have breeched so irresponsibly—no, so diabolically.

But as days gathered into weeks, routine life on the reserve, with some necessary adjustments, fell into place. Morose, I simply went about my business, despite the permanent lump in my crop—and my weeping insomnia.

Late at night, without warning, Madeline would appear to me. She looked so beautiful and so defenseless, her black eyes darting about in innocent confusion, the horror yet to unfold. Then I would watch helplessly as the deadly, orange beaks plunged down on her. Scene followed scene—I could not stop any of it—as my mind replayed the insane transformation in the grove from Father's funeral to Madeline's execution. At some point, out of emotional exhaustion, I would finally drop into sleep—but then, vivid, ghastly nightmares would pick up where conscious memory left off.

Every night was bad. As soon as the evening light began to fade, I would slip my head under a wing, desperate for sleep, for oblivion. In that black cocoon, above the muffled quacking of the ducks in the cove I could hear my pulse throbbing. Immediately, my heartbeat would quicken, my body already sensing and growing fearful of the murder scenes my torment was about to thrust again on stage.

I would try to shove back against the visions, but it was like swimming against rapids. The effort made my skin tighten and my feet would paddle spontaneously—absurdly—as if it were possible to escape, so that I would sometimes find myself bobbing in rough water outside the lee of the cove.

In the morning, my guilt would be waiting to greet me. It climbed on my back and I would carry it around all day, as if it were a dead loon chick. The past cannot be shed. There was no mercy.

Mother, her grief fading, took to her daily tasks with composure, if not cheer. Harold took on the role of her guardian. He shadowed her, swam in her wake, and floated reassuringly at her side when she finally resumed her bedtime stories.

Mother, without protest, accepted these attentions, as if she and Harold both understood that it was the appropriate time for filial duty to be reversed.

Troy, having renounced fermies, directed his ambitious nature to revival, and at an even higher pitch than when he had left the reserve to lead the migration. He turned fervently religious and political. He had himself Phoenixated and attended every one of Pastor Jasper's services. Sensing an opportunity to champion a resolution of differences on the reserve, he got it in his mind to seek the office of king.

"Bloedel is in chaos, my brother," Troy told me in a newly adopted voice, a kind of gruff quack, which he perhaps thought gave the impression of rugged conviction, but actually seemed to render him less intelligent. "And no one is stepping up to prevent certain disaster," he warned. "I've watched the players, seen how it's done, learned from my missteps. I can turn things around, Marcel—redeem myself through public service. It's what Father would have wanted for me, to finish what he started. It's family destiny, Phoenix be praised."

Troy's renewed fervor was goaded on by Pastor Jasper, who, apparently detecting in my brother the potential to promote his own agenda, now encouraged his sobriety.

"I sense in you the will of the Phoenix, Troy," he cheered, perched cajolingly on the dead log in our cove.

"You know, Pastor, when I left on migration, I had visions of forging a new life, free of dissent and strife," Troy said, his eyes lit by new fire, "but it was premature. I'll be the first to admit I wasn't ready. I can see that now. Fact is, I didn't have to go anywhere. My calling was right here all the time, here on the reserve."

"Carpe diem, my boy," Pastor Jasper whistled. "Carp, trout, mute, tundra—I'll be disappointed—crestfallen—if we don't hook 'em all!"

It's hard not to admire aspiration, especially among family. I looked at my brother, his head held high. I wished I had half his ambition.

Pastor Jasper bestowed his blessing and flew off. High above, a broad formation of Canada geese dotted the sky, crossing to the south. Troy quietly watched them pass. "They're heading somewhere new and exciting, Marcel, " he said. "But not all of them will make it. This time, I will."

That evening, Mother told one of my favorite stories, the tale of D'buque Duck, how, long ago, at the beginning of time, the Creator brought forth the first duck or duck egg—no one is sure which came first, actually—and either placed or hatched this duck in a certain idyllic bird sanctuary, warm and wet and peaceful, with an abundance of the most tender tubers and es-cargot. Her name was D'buque and the Creator gave her total reign over the vast reserve. After a time, though, D'buque grew lonely, and so the Creator removed one of her feathers, respect-ing her wish to take it from where the gap wouldn't show, and from the feather the Creator made her a mate, which she was allowed to name and to decorate with colors of her own choos-ing, a scheme considerably less dull than she thought the Cre-ator could have been willing to risk on herself—"A nice, jazzy green head would be nice," she decided. She named her mate Evan.

The Creator, seeing how D'buque's loneliness had now been dealt with, appointed her general custodian, on condi-tion she agree not to roam outside the reserve.

The pair had everything they could ask for, until one day Evan said to D'buque, "You know, there is so much space here, dear, we could rent out half of it and still not feel crowded."

"Who would we rent to?" asked D'buque. "We're the only ducks in the world."

Overcoming her objection that she had promised not to set wing off the reserve, Evan convinced D'buque that a bit of scouting just outside its boundaries would not cause any harm and might quickly produce some tenants, which they could thereafter join socially to liven up their rather quiet and predictable lives.

However, no sooner had D'buque and Evan launched across the reserve's border than the terrain beneath them turned strange and foreboding. The sweet, humid air of the reserve suddenly blasted hot and dry, searing their throats. Their eyes itched and their flesh burned. Weird creatures prowled the earth below, making a landing unthinkable. Reversing course, they saw that the reserve had vanished, and that the same arid, alien landscape stretched to the four horizons. They sent distress calls, but of course there were no ducks to answer.

Hunger and thirst soon forced D'buque and Evan to land. They chose a place on a half-evaporated lake of brackish water, around which at least some coarse, barely edible vegetation had sprouted. Working purely from survival instinct, D'buque enlightened Evan and they produced two eggs, which she incubated into the first generation of our ancestors. A drake and a duck hatched, and in their hearts was sealed a deep longing for the perfection of the sanctuary their parents had once enjoyed, a longing that has been passed down generation to generation.

At this point, Mother would rest and survey her spellbound listeners. Then she would take a deep breath and close with, "Some say that our lost primal sanctuary still exists and that it is home to the Phoenix and to the souls of our departed, which, upon expiry, are gathered and escorted there by a guide. Bless you all."

And so would the evening have ended. But this time, Mother added a heartbroken quack and said, "Before you leave, Pastor Jasper has asked to say a few words."

There was Pastor Jasper, flitting in the purple twilight from perch to perch on the log. He settled on the stub of a branch and cleared his throat. "Dear family and friends, it is only when tragedy strikes hardest that we understand the truth of what before were only entertaining stories. We may all rejoice, knowing our beloved Basil and Madeline have made their final, holy migration—together, in this divine happenstance, and we know how Basil always did yearn to migrate somewhere—the journey to the sanctuary of the Phoenix."

Here, he allowed for a wave of sobbing to ebb, sending me a glance of impatience when mine didn't.

"And, we must recognize that after grief has made its painful visit, life resumes, problems and all—which is why I asked to speak with you this evening, and I am honored to have been given this opportunity," he said, flicking a solemn nod at Mother, "thanks to Doris' graciousness."

As if on cue, Troy separated himself from the others and swam briskly to the log. I saw Harold roll his eyes up.

Pastor Jasper inflated his breast, its crimson curve rusty in the fading light. "My dear brothers and sisters," he exhaled, "we have endured so much misfortune this past year—none of it deserved, but, I suggest, entirely the result of a deficit of morally inspired political leadership. For too long we have lacked a king. For too long, no bird has risen to the challenge of uniting us. Now, before us floats Troy, the brave and devout progeny of our stalwart drake Basil, may he rest in heaven with the Phoenix."

Troy, bobbing with a grave set to his bill, lowered his head in a gesture of noblesse oblige and gave the water a humble twirl.

"This evening," Pastor Jasper piped as he leapt up to flutter around Troy, "I announce to you my total commitment to the election of Troy to the office of…King of Bloedel Reserve!"

Confused quacking rose from the cove. There were a few raucous cheers. Then Uncle Arthur's raspy voice rose through the din. "Troy? King? With all due respect, Pastor, I hope you both have not been partaking of the holy refreshment. I dearly love my nephew, but he has not recently displayed what I would call a model of sensible leadership—least not in public, anyways, excuse my bluntness."

This produced some nervous titters among the flock, as Uncle Arthur's candor usually did.

Pastor Jasper did not have time to fashion a reply or even leap clear before Troy flapped into an erect posture in the water. "Uncle Arthur," he quacked, heedless that the spray from his wings was dousing Jasper's perch, "I'm sure I'm speaking for our pastor when I say that we're not going to take that remark personally..."

"Well, you should," Uncle Arthur broke in, "if you want to avoid deceiving yourselves."

Troy overrode him in a testy voice. "...because it's the future of the reserve that's at stake here—our freedom, and..."

This time, Troy was interrupted by Pastor Jasper, who had flitted a couple of circles overhead to dry off and collect himself. He disliked marsh water. "Now Arthur," he piped, "no one is ever going to accuse you of speaking in euphemisms, and we do appreciate your calling attention to some very valid concerns in this matter."

"Might as well put a scarecrow in charge," Uncle Arthur said. "Or Marcel, here."

Just the mention of my name in a public gathering made me wither inside myself, not to mention the roar of painful laughter that Uncle Arthur drew from the crowd. But to my relief, Pastor Jasper was good at handling objectors and didn't spare me a glance. However, he did hop a few wingspans upwind of Troy, who had settled back into a stately float.

Pastor Jasper let the chuckles die down, rejoining with his charismatic warble. "Arthur, I would think you would be proud to see a mallard—and a relative at that—bring peace to our land, someone to get both sides of the isle to cooperate. You wouldn't stand apart from your own kind, would you?"

Yes, apart from my own kind—there, I was jolted to think, is exactly where *I* stood. You reach a point where you can look back and see how your path through life has left only a trail of problems for others to clean up—and not a single thing of value amid the debris to repay their magnanimity. I had no doubt that my failed life had disappointed Father. Moreover, I would never be able to escape the knowledge that in exchange for the gift of life, I had served him death. Just as Troy had stolen the quill from me, hadn't I, purely in my own interests, stolen Father from Mother?

And as for Madeline, in payment for the joy she had brought me, she had had to suffer first barrenness and then annihilation. With the clarity of these facts, the full brunt of my unpardonable sins rocked me.

As I watched bills and beaks open and close, the voices of Pastor Jasper, Troy and the others merged into a cacophony of quacks and whistles and their words blended into gibberish. Only the punishing thoughts in my head rang clear. It now became obvious that all the other birds, despite the frictions of life, managed to dwell together as a community, while I lived outside. I realized that I was the only adult duck in the cove without a role, and I understood at last why I felt such affinity with Louis, the paragon of loners.

I did not want to live like this. I did not want to suffer every night with my head under my wing while the chronicle of destruction that I had brought upon my family and flock passed in review. I decided that in the morning, I would paddle out to the east side of the lake and offer myself to the otters. If I could not benefit my own kind, I could at least relieve them of a burden—and, as penance, provide a meal for another creature.

Having made this pact with myself, I felt refreshed, even elated, as if I had awoken from a long, deep sleep. I looked about at the generations of ducks floating around me and felt an unfamiliar kinship with them, the kind of esteem, I realized, that you can only feel as an equal. By sundown tomorrow, they would know I had redeemed myself. The slate would be wiped clean.

To end the gathering, Pastor Jasper led a prayer for Troy's success, and everyone dispersed. The owls and frogs started up. The full moon rinsed our cove with a cleansing light. I found my spot near the log and took a deep breath of relief before slipping my head under my wing. The wind was from the north and the air was stringent with pine. There were no visions that night, no nightmares. I felt as if the ghosts of wounded souls were finally departing.

Chapter 12

Dawn broke, laying liquid red pigment on the horizon. Rain was coming. The clean emptiness of morning hunger felt right. I would not need breakfast. I was ready.

I decided against a farewell visit to Louis. I had not yet thanked him for defending us against the mutes at the funeral, despite the tragic outcome, but he would sense what I was about to do and try to talk me out of it. My resolve was frail, I knew, and I was too easily persuaded. I could not allow myself to bungle my last chance for redemption.

I especially regretted not making time to thank Louis for his most beautiful song, which had burrowed into my psyche, waiting, ready for the final moment. Making time is another thing I was never good at—inserting my presence into the proper moment, that is. Time is always streaming along, of course, and any moment is as good as another for diving in, but it was as if my anxiety had always kept me standing on its banks, so to speak, afraid to jump, as if there wouldn't be room for me. But like water, there is always room in time.

I set out to the east, paddling at a relaxed pace, so as not to attract attention. After a while, I stopped and looked back. There was our cove, cupping the morning light, family and flock slumbering there like little bumps on the water, the grove rising behind.

A pang of wistfulness stabbed my gut. "I can't decide which I love more," Madeline used to sigh, "panoramas or escargot." She would look at me and ask, "Which do you think I like best, Marcel?" I had learned to dodge questions like that. But the fun of romantic play didn't matter to me any more.

I shouldn't have stopped. Stopping sprang a leak in my courage. It gave me time to feel stranded. My distance from the safety of the cove, now in perspective, was alarming, and the dangerous expanse of lake ahead sent a chill down my spine. In one of Mother's stories, a duck looked back and was turned into a log of salt—not that it would matter if I turned to salt, except to disappoint the otters. But like most of Mother's stories, it served to illustrate a failure of discipline, always my weakest quality.

The wind was picking up ahead of the rain. I bobbed up and down, watching gusts spread whitecaps across the lake. It would be hard to see an approaching otter in the rough water, and that was good—better to go unexpectedly.

I forged ahead. Slowly, the eastern shoreline drew closer. I was tempted to launch and fly the remaining distance, but I was sure I would be too afraid to land if I saw an otter from aloft. The scent in the air seemed to change—perhaps more mammalian. Bits of debris drifted by, and each one to me was a black nose. My heart started to pound. I could make out the edge of the lake and what looked like holes in the raised bank, out of which otters must have already slipped as they saw me coming—the more the better, I thought, to get it over with.

I tried to compose myself. My pulse pounded in my head. Now was the time to bring forth Louis's song. I hunted to find the special place where I kept it.

The song was gone. I could not recall it. Like buzzing grasshoppers, all manner of other music hopped into my ears—everything from crow satire to seductive dove lyrics. But Louis' song had hidden itself away. It would not come. My eternal last moment of bliss threatened to turn into a torture chamber of fear, regret and self-recrimination. I started to panic.

The freshening wind had shifted and was propelling me faster toward the shore. Time was running out. I strained to find just the first notes of Louis' song, praying that they might worm into the divine cache where the full, uplifting composition had hidden itself. But it was as if the moon had disappeared behind a black overcast.

A terrific splash burst in front of me, the spray tinted red in the sun. I screamed at the top of my lungs.

"Marcel, don't scare me like that!" Troy squawked. "What in Phoenix's name are you doing out here all by yourself?"

I couldn't catch my breath to answer.

"In about another minute, you'll be otter fodder." He looked about warily.

"That's the idea," I gasped, finally, giddy and almost unhinged by fright.

"Come on, Marcel, let's launch and get out of here. I'm getting a bit nervous being so close to the shore."

"Leave me alone, Troy," I resisted, starting to regain some composure and recalling my original intention. "I'm committing suicide."

"What?"

"Suicide," I repeated. "Killing myself." I tried to muster some pride in my voice, but it sounded hollow even to me.

"You're not serious."

"You wouldn't happen to remember the first few notes of that song Louis sang at Father's funeral, would you?"

Troy gave me a worried look. "Come on Marcel, we can't stay here. Let's go home"

It was over—suddenly, I snapped free of the grip of whatever had driven me to this. Maybe the word "home" did it, or the way Troy said it, an uncommon softness in his voice—I don't know, but my muscles went slack. I couldn't move. "I'd like to do that, Troy," I said.

"Well, then, let's go."

"I can't."

"Listen, we'll talk, I'll tell you all about the migration. Whatever you want. Let's just get going, all right?"

"I mean I can't launch. I'm petrified—paralyzed or something."

Wings beating, Troy lunged forward, nipping at my tail feathers, just as Father had done when we were ducklings learning to fly. I scooted ahead with a squawk and took to the air. If I ever got to heaven, I would ask the Phoenix if I could keep my wings.

Chapter 13

"You should have said something," Troy scolded me from the lead position. "You'd have been a dead duck by now if I hadn't noticed you out there." We were crossing over Louis' island, angling home, cold rain starting to spit. I looked for the familiar white berry on a stem. It was conspicuously—astonishingly—absent. Louis had apparently vacated.

"I just let myself be caught up in things, Troy." I peered back, trying to locate Louis.

"It's just pure good luck that Jasper sent me out to check on what the tundras were up to. First time he did that."

Pure good luck is probably the most perfect gift of all—undeserved, no strings attached. Below, Clout's red canoe was tied at the dock and his green truck was backed up to the observation deck. In the truck bed was a cage, and, banking left, I could see something white and large inside the cage.

"Troy," I called, my concern rising. "Down at the deck—Clout's truck!"

"I'll tell Jasper I didn't have time to check on the tundras."

"I think Louis is in that cage."

"Jasper'll be irked, but I'll get to it first thing in the morning. Nothing's going to change overnight, I'll say."

"If it's Louis, he could be gone in another minute!"

"Marcel, enough for today, okay? It's almost dinnertime and I'm starved."

The mention of dinner brought my stomach to life. My tongue tingled. I had never felt so famished. With the rain, the slugs would be out in profusion. But food could wait a bit longer if Louis was in trouble.

I rolled out, setting my course for the truck.

Troy caught up from behind. "Darn it, Marcel, I'm the leader here."

I thrust out my wings to brake, felt my shoulder tendons bracing taut across my breast, and hovered upright into a precision landing on top of the cage.

Troy swooped past, barking out, "You're on your own, now, but I expect to see you at the cove in half an hour. Don't make me come back for you."

"I won't be a minute, Troy," I promised, something telling me not to be so quick pledging the unknown future, "—and thanks."

"I'm going to speak with Jasper about some counseling for you," he called back. "If you want to get on the straight and narrow, he's the one to trust."

A familiar but wheezy voice escaped from the cage. "Dear me, have you departed from the straight and narrow, Marcel?"

"Louis!" I quacked. "You *are* in there."

"Did I not foretell that Clout had a plan for me?" Louis' voice resonated through the wet boards under my feet, reminding me of the throaty heron from Sorghum, but less healthy.

Except for Clout's leg-banding obsession, it seemed impossible to fathom what humans thought about birds, yet I had to admit that Louis had intuited something. "We must get you out, Louis," I squawked—too loud, as if the wire mesh door were solid steel. "What's wrong with your voice?"

"Only a bit of congestion—one hopes,'" Louis croaked, his eyes rheumy, his aura rough at the edges. "But tell me what have you been up to—something to do with your recent loss, no doubt." He adjusted the set of his wings and stared at me with his unflappable gaze. "Which I'm sorry for, Marcel. Sorry it was all begun, authored, so to speak, by those blasted pinions. Unforgivable — the tragedy those quills brought about, how they found their way from me to you, almost fatefully. But you should have come to see me before you did something rash—whatever it was."

There was no time to discuss what had happened. Dropping to the open tailgate of the truck, I peered through the grill into the dim cage, where Louis's white form filled the interior with an alabaster glow. It was as if Clout had decided to make Louis's self-imprisonment official, to assume control of it. Or perhaps Louis had unknowingly violated some human law and was now being sentenced. I had always believed that Louis would eventually reconcile with his disability, release himself from his island and rejoin our community. Now, it was out of his wings.

"Where is Clout taking you?" I quacked, trying to focus on the present.

"One must get to the bottom of one's pain, Marcel. Then, one must detach," Louis coughed, his eyes closing to slits. "Images of your dead father, of Madeline—you must bring them closer, closer, closer and then release them. There is too much anguish in life for any one bird to hold on to." His eyes opened, fixed on me with a filmy intensity. "Recall when your uncle Blake landed on the high-tension lines—one must let go of loss before one is burned up by it — like the Phoenix."

Scenes of the carnage at the funeral flashed before my eyes. I felt the scars on my abdomen tighten and winced. I looked at Louis in his cage and suddenly glimpsed the rot of life in detention — cut off from a future, at the mercy of bad memories. But at least imprisonment spares one, I suppose, from having to make further decisions that could lead to more pain.

Decisions were never my forte. I had always so looked forward to the end of the day, to a story, then sleep—freedom from choosing what to do with myself next. At dawn, the morning rays would prod and probe but I would procrastinate, consider the possibilities, test all potential repercussions, work my nerves into a dither over doing the wrong thing—that is, until had I decided on suicide.

I heard human voices approaching. I hopped down from the tailgate and crouched on the deck, ready to launch.

"Marcel, Melody will be worried. Do get a message to her." Louis called out, probably thinking—as I had moved out of his line of sight—that I had fled. "Tell her I think Clout's taking me to Sorghum."

Sorghum! But before I could utter a quack, Clout strode up to the truck, the woman with the binoculars close behind under an umbrella. He raised the tailgate and they got in and slammed the doors. A puff of blue smoke blew out of the pipe at the back as the truck started up and roared off, bouncing out of sight around a curve.

I launched and climbed above the trees in time to see the truck accelerate past the mansion and out the main gate, Chief Wachu restraining his tomahawk as the kidnappers sped through the gate, Louis a white smudge framed in the cage door. The clouds had dropped very low, and when I tried to climb higher to track the course of the truck on the highway, I found myself wrapped in thick, blinding mist. Descending, I skimmed between clouds and treetops, pursuing the truck as best I could for a good twenty minutes, until my speed began to flag from hunger, the yellow glow of the headlights fading to the north.

The pursuit, brief as it was, galvanized my sense of purpose. And, although my gizzard felt as hollow as a dried deer skull, the fact that Louis had entrusted me with a mission—to deliver his message to Melody—made hunger seem a pesky inconvenience.

Leaning hard into a turn, I swung back toward the reserve. Although I knew the magnetic direction, the lack of familiar ground references gave me a twinge of apprehension. But as I flapped, the black road materialized steadily out of the cloaking mist, drawing me on, as if it could be forever relied upon for guidance.

The road gave me the same sense of imprint as I'd had seven years before, as a duckling following Mother. Only now as I flew, I had a strange sense of observing myself flying. It was as if I were two mallards—myself, and a double that was flying simultaneously above, below and all around me, watching me, and somehow sending its observations into my brain. "That's good, Marcel," the double seemed to be saying. "Keep going."

Perhaps because she had never had to compromise with a mate on design or construction, nor sit a brood, Melody's nest was architecturally distinct. A rampart of interlaced sticks faced the lake, sweeping back into a highly defensible fortification of twigs daubed with mud, as otter-proof as anything I'd seen on the reserve, except, of course, Clout's cabin and the mansion—the way humans barricade themselves in. From the air, Melody could be seen ensconced in her nest facing the open water, scanning for threats. She had her father's exalted bearing and toughness and her mother's serene graciousness.

"Why, Marcel," she greeted me as I slid in for a water landing, "it must be a family outing in all this rain. I just saw your brothers heading out to the east—in a jolly good hurry, too."

"Brothers?" When I didn't return to the cove, Troy must have thought I was determined to be otter fodder!

"Clout has abducted *your* brother," I quacked.

"Abducted? Louis?" Her neck arched back in surprise. "Strange, come to think of it, I did *feel* something from him a while ago—it woke me up."

"In Clout's truck—in a cage. They went north. On the road to the ferry. You have to do something!" Torn between emergencies, I felt my heart pounding. "Listen, I have to go. Troy thinks I'm being eaten by an otter."

"But when he's been thinking too hard, my brother often gets quite roiled up under that calm exterior of his, so I didn't think anything of it," she said, looking off in the direction of Louis' island. "Oh, my—Clout, you say?"

"Just say you'll do something!"

She turned to me with a kindly gaze. "You are in a dither, love. What's all this about otters? You're quite safe here with me."

"Well, I tried to…oh, it's too hard to explain, Melody. I really have to go."

"Do hurry, then. Best to Troy and Harold, and your mum, of course, and mind the otters." She had risen to her feet and begun to flex her mighty wings. "They went north to the ferry, you say?" Her black eyes shone. "What on earth would Clout want with him now?"

"And Louis said to tell you they were taking him to Sorghum."

"Sorghum?"

"Actually, he seemed a bit sick," I said, my eye catching a cluster of five escargot at the foot of Melody's nest. She must have gathered them for dinner.

Melody followed my gaze. "Oh, of course, help yourself, Marcel—I'm quite full and they'll only escape. You look famished, my dear."

She shook her wings, producing a fluttering thunder, and peered off across the lake. "Sorghum," she sighed. "Louis can be such a bother, but I am quite fond of him, you know. 'No need to be so tragic about it, dear,' I told him when he was pinioned, but one's heart does go out—frightful thing to happen in one's prime, really." She watched me gobbling up the escargot. "There's something in some birds that begs to be rescued, Marcel, and if we must, we must, mustn't we?"

The royal "we" can be confusing, but I hadn't time to ask questions. Melody would rescue Louis just as Troy had saved me. I knew I could depend upon her.

Recharged with food, I excused myself and launched to the east, setting a course just above the choppy surface of the lake, where my brothers would be able to pick me out from above. Sure enough, in a matter of minutes I saw the unmistakable silhouettes of two ducks against the clouds.

"Great Phoenix, Marcel, you had us all in a panic," Troy squawked as he drew alongside.

"I'm sorry, Troy, but Clout took Louis away, and I…"

"We didn't dare tell mother where we were going," Harold interrupted, "or why—it would've killed her."

Troy took the lead and began a climbing turn back to the cove. From the north shore came a cheerful trumpet as Melody spotted us. "Sleep well! Departing in the morning!" she called.

I felt reassured. She was strong, and despite that we were of different species I had always nurtured a special regard for her. Like all leaders, at each fork in the way she would lunge unhesitatingly and cheerfully ahead, relying on quick, mature instincts.

It occurred to me then how cheerfulness and strength always seemed to go as a pair, like wings. And just as suddenly the thought struck me—what would have been the effect on Mother had I succeeded in killing myself? My stomach turned in self-revulsion. Despondency and weakness, that other inseparable pair, were the wings I had flown on.

Back in the cove, the fullness of coming home swelled in my heart. Mother, sensing trouble but not knowing the extent, greeted me with open wings. Uncle Arthur gave me an uncharacteristic fraternal, husky quack as he passed. Troy and Harold gathered some exceedingly tender reeds and a slug big enough to choke a heron.

I had done more than enough for one day. In the morning, there would be better things to look forward to than execution by otter. What is it that can take control of one's mind like that? Safely surrounded again by family, a numbing fatigue fell over me. Every muscle ached and the roots of my feathers burned dully. My body felt like the dead log mired near my sleeping spot. At the edge of slumber, my eyelids weighted shut, I thought about Louis—how no one except Melody and I would care if he disappeared forever. He had cut himself off from everyday life, to cohabitate with his pain, as if it were a secret mistress. After Madeline's and Father's deaths, I knew how it felt to be seduced by pain. Melody understood, too. She would bring Louis back. I had done what I could for him. I felt my double hovering near, saw myself from above, heard his question—"Have you?"

Chapter 14

I sensed her presence in my slumber, and the feeling of her there spawned dreams—shards of light glinting off iridescent surfaces that seemed to be made of water, feathers and crystal all at the same time, that somehow seemed to be parts of me, as well.

I felt her fierce resolve fix on me like an eagle's stare, burning through what I had pretended to myself—that Melody's royal "we" did not include me.

"Marcel, it's time to go," she was saying, and her words splintered into music, then the notes merged with white sparks, swirling together.

"We'll have some breakfast, Marcel and then be on our way," the sparks and music said. "It's a long way, dear."

My eyelids strained open. Melody floated before me, huge, white and loftily composed.

"Louis should have resisted," she was saying, "but that's the way he is—taciturn as Chief Wachu, I'm afraid, and stoic as a ...oh, what's the use, we'll simply have to go and find him."

"Go?" My groggy brain tried to put together what it was being told but dropped its preliminary conclusion like a gull letting go a too-heavy fish—although it did hang on to the word "breakfast."

"I've rounded up some escargot and I'm sure we'll find a decent cuisine en route. I'll just paddle over to say bonjour and au revoir to Doris while we're shaking the sleep from our eyes, love."

"En route?" I quacked dreamily. "We?"

"Character is savoir faire," Father used to pronounce. "A mallard's character is chipped out bit by bit by the decisions he makes, son. Fish and cut debate, I say."

But I lacked even a grain of savoir faire—knowing what to say, what to do and when. It was my habit to go with the flow. Flowing was my character. Looking back to that time and place in our cove, it seemed ordained, therefore, that I, the pliant Marcel, would follow Melody.

She waited while I made ready to leave. "Au revoir!" I remember quacking to Mother, mimicking the casual tone with which Melody had just bade farewell—"See you soon!"

Mother floated solemnly, bridling her usual farewell—an overdramatic sweep of the wing and a grand, "Adieu!"

"Do be careful," she whispered, this time, "Phoenix bless, dear." With an uneasy glance at Melody, she gave me a nuzzle. "You'll be in capable wings with her, Marcel." She back-paddled a few strokes, as if to squarely frame me in her memory. "Your father would have been proud, I'm sure." She gazed up into the morning sky. "Is proud," she amended.

The notion of Father's pride in me sent a shiver of joy down my back.

Turning to Melody, Mother asked, "Where exactly are you going to look for Louis?"

I had not mentioned Sorghum to anyone but Melody.

"Doesn't matter, Mother, it'll broaden his horizons," Troy shouldered in, perhaps genuinely in hope that a purposeful adventure would be healthy for me—and, conceivably, pricked by the shame of his failed migration. "Drakes are meant to explore the world, I'm here to tell. I'd join them if I hadn't pledged myself to my future constituents on the reserve." He paused, allowing Melody, whose steely self-confidence dominated the scene, a moment to appreciate the gravity of his commitment. Then he turned to me. "Good luck, Marcel. Mind the otters, now."

"Louis ain't worth your life," Uncle Arthur grunted, "excusing my bluntness."

"Have some nice escargot, Arthur," Mother said. "Melody brought them."

"Snails give me gas," Uncle Arthur said.

Following Melody went beyond mustering the courage to leave my family. Yes, I would join her in pursuit of Louis — her brother and my best friend—but still as Uncle Arthur pointed out, a decision worth thinking twice about. But I selfishly sensed that there was something in it for me. I naturally expected to return to see my family again. Doesn't every bird, upon setting out upon a journey? At the same time, with the mysterious Sorghum waiting in the wings, I felt a tremor of providence stir in my gizzard, a whispered promise of opportunity — to redeem myself from all transgression, perhaps like a wayward young swan conscript facing his first battle, his chance to earn salvation, by victory or death.

Here was the chance to challenge my wings and find their limits, to free myself from my chronic fear, which seemed to well up in me simply as a result of inching forward with my life, the way ripples are generated as a consequence of swimming—this bloodsucking fear that was coupled with a compulsive need to berate myself for it.

Melody and I said our goodbyes, breakfasted well, and launched from the lake in dead-calm air — a high, luminous overcast, through which could be seen a heatless disc of sun. Below, the water lay dark and flat as an oil slick. Ahead, visibility was clear and sharp, the sky arching cavernous and infinite above the far, jagged, snowy peaks of the Olympics. Melody set a course west by northwest, directly at the mountains. From behind, a few cheering honks and squawks rose from the lake, fading as we settled into a rhythm paced for distance.

We followed the road north, away from the Bainbridge Island port. In a short time, the coast, rimmed with human habitation, curved before us like a great paw. The docks, spiking out like claws, dug into the bay. Beyond, Puget Sound spread out broad and gray, small islands riding through the chop, while farther north, the dark green Gulf Islands mounded handsomely on the horizon. Half a dozen ferryboats with white tails of wake affixed astern crisscrossed the sea, tracking invisible lines between the islands, as small maelstroms of gulls wheeled above their decks.

As we crossed the shoreline, I noted that my reach from home had extended farther than ever before. I felt a bubble of misgiving rise in my abdomen, but it was not the usual crippling dismay, that wrench of premature defeat. It was more like the alarming sensation of height the first time I flew—precarious and exciting.

I flew in the wash of Melody's powerful wings, slightly to her left, taking advantage of eddies of air that curled behind her and helped to tug me along. I had almost forgotten the purpose of our journey. The thrill of being underway now seemed reason enough to have left all else behind. I saw us through the eyes of my double: a powerful trumpeter driving forward above the rugged landscape, an ordinary but willing mallard in tow. We were on an odyssey.

"This must be what it feels like to migrate," I quacked to Melody.

"By the time we get to the other side, we'll want to find something to eat," she called back. "That's basically what migration is all about, dear."

Her pragmatism roused me from my romanticizing. "What is on the other side, Melody?"

"The main thing now is the hunters, dear. It's the season. They put decoys out in the best feeding coves."

I had heard about hunters. They had guns that killed at a distance and I knew that decoys could be fatally realistic. More than one of my cousins had succumbed.

"And they won't be swan decoys, my dear," Melody warned. "You'll think it's your family down there."

"I'll be careful," I said.

"Hunters are good at hiding. They watch the sky from their blinds. By the way we fly, they'll know you're a duck and they'll think I'm a goose—both of us fair game. So stay with me on this, love. Not let our stomachs overrule our brains, shall we?"

Since the previous day, I thought I now knew much more about controlling my impulses. It was hard to believe that only twenty-four hours ago I might have jumped at the idea of being shot by a hunter.

"And as for what's on the other side, I've never explored this far west, frankly, but we'll find out when we get there, as they say," Melody laughed. "I do know it's part of the peninsula. We're headed for those mountains—that's where Sorghum is supposed to be, or whatever name that place goes by these days."

That place? It seemed to me that the time had come at last to learn the facts about Sorghum. It was after all our destination. I could number only three times in my life when the name of the place had come up—twice in my brush with the green heron at the funerals and once after Troy's nightmare. When I thought about it, I wasn't even certain that Louis was being taken there. How would Louis have known what Clout had in mind?

"How would Louis know Clout was taking him to Sorghum, Melody?" I called.

"Sorghum is just an expression, dear."

"An expression for what? I thought it was a place."

"Well, it could be that, too."

"I don't understand."

"Look, the coast is coming up already."

Before us, the eastern coast of the peninsula barricaded the sea. A segmented white strand marked where the surf broke upon its desolate beaches. The chain of mountains had drawn closer, revealing the texture of pines that feathered the slopes up to the tree line—striated wedges of granite reaching even higher.

"It all looks a bit scary," I said.

"It's claimed there's a big sanctuary in those foothills ahead—partway up the base of that high peak. It's supposed to be a bit weird—humans doing strange experiments and goodness knows what else. Pinioning, at least. Some birds do call it Sorghum, but I don't credit it. Sorghum is really where the Phoenix is supposed to live—with the souls of the dead, as you must know, dear. It's claimed you can get closer and closer to where the Phoenix is but never actually get there. A lot have tried, a lot have died, the saying goes. Your brother, Troy, was lucky, according to Jasper."

"What happened to Troy?"

"You should ask him yourself, dear."

"I've tried."

"The gossip says he was lured away from the migration."

"Lured?"

"By a heron, supposedly." She looked away, as if some indecency were occurring. "Actually, I detest gossip."

At the mention of a heron, my rhythm broke and I stumbled out of formation, dropping through Melody's wake, and I had to pump hard to climb back to the spot where I could cruise in her draft. I felt my mind busily thatching together bits of information, like a nest—a nest for whom or what, I wasn't sure.

"All scurrilous hearsay, but it may have been a hoopoe, not a heron," she went on, gliding a beat or two to let me catch up, "although I've never seen one of those—cross between a peacock and a curlew, I hear. Whichever, the offer of utopia is the bait—Sorghum, for those of the Phoenix persuasion, or somewhere in Egypt, the Horus priests claim…in the West Nile, I recall…or was it Persia? For Louis, though, I think going to Sorghum was just a bit of his wry humor."

I tried to concentrate. "What about the souls of the dead?"

"What would you like to know?"

"Would Madeline be there? And Father? And Phoebe? And your parents?"

"When the outlook is darkest, dear, the spirit may curl up in hibernation but not in extinction. Deep down, it remains as fertile for hope as an unmated gander for a goose. The slightest hint of the possibility of renewal can wake it up."

At this, I was rocked by the conviction that Pastor Jasper was right—Heaven was an inarguable reality. It was obvious. The Creator could not have failed to set aside a special province in the universe where the departed would stay and where they would be waiting for you when your own time came.

Therefore, I reasoned, such a place as Sorghum must, beyond all shadow of doubt, exist. Sorghum must be a special zone, like a migratory stop or the human's observation deck on the reserve, to where, given the right instructions, a living relative could travel—as a visitor, to meet with departed loved ones. Clout must be taking Louis there to meet Edward and Veronica. At Sorghum, I would also find Madeline and Father and all my lost relatives.

By this logic, the torn seams of my love began to fuse, to heal, and I perceived the most irreconcilable parts of existence commence to join together—the past and the future—promising to make whole and forever my connection with the ones dear to me. I felt as if a stand of trees had been felled by a bolt of lightning and behind them, blocked from view until that moment, stood a vision of eternal paradise.

I felt light-headed, my breathing relaxed, power surged from my heart into my muscles. I drew alongside Melody, radiating gratitude and affection.

"My, and I thought you might be needing some sustenance by now," she said. "Well, to answer your question, it is lovely to think that our deceased loved ones are waiting for us somewhere, dear."

"I don't think, Melody. I know."

"Well, that's all it takes, then."

"I'm so glad I came with you."

"Quite." She glanced at me. "Your eyes are blazing, dear."

We were directly above the coast, marking the end of the gray uniformity of the sea and the resumption of the varied and intricate perils of land. Melody stopped flapping and pitched down toward a small recess in the shoreline, vegetation skinned well back from a beach of dark gravel.

"See that little cove below? Follow me. Not much cover there for hunters, but you never know. Be ready to take evasive action."

Descending in a straight glide, Melody abruptly pulled up, swerved right, then left, then right again. "Mustn't make an easy target, dear. I don't see anything amiss, though—no decoys, and the brush looks too skimpy to conceal a human."

She plummeted down, I chasing, and I saw our reflections loom up and erupt in salt spray as we skimmed to a landing on the glassy surface of the cove.

"Superb, dear," Melody declared. "Let's check the menu down here. Ah, there's a bit of smartweed for you just up the beach in front of those ferns—tasty, and it takes the edge off when one can't wait another minute for a mollusk. I'm going to hunt up some escargot for us. I have a yen for tadpoles, too, but they're out of season, aren't they."

My stomach signaled its approval with a gurgle but my mind still raced with thoughts of Sorghum "We won't have to stop long, will we, Melody?"

"We're experiencing the Response, aren't we, dear."

I looked at her, wondering if I could express the urgency I was feeling. "Just anxious to reach Sorghum."

"If Jasper saw your eyes right now, he'd have you Phoenix-ated on the spot—sprinkled with holy sand, blessed and sent out on recruitment."

"I know we have to eat, Melody. It's just that something occurred to me and I put together some things you said about Sorghum and a green heron and…"

"Oh, dear, not that old green heron that flies in for all the funerals." She gave me a sympathetic sigh. "Nests on the other side of the island. A croak like doomsday—scares other birds half to death when they first hear it. He's quite harmless, though."

I briefly considered this information, which kicked at one of the legs of my freshly hatched revelation but failed to bring it down. "Sometimes you just know something."

"Well, of course, dear, that's what the Response is all about."

"Please don't condescend, Melody. I want to help you find Louis, but now there's more involved than just him."

"Not a jot of condescension, Marcel." She turned her head to one side in order to look me in the eye. "There are many things we just *know* to be true. And of course life eventually will reveal to us which ones really are true and which are false, if we allow it. But the big questions can only be answered after death, you see—makes patience the greatest virtue, doesn't it. Don't expect too much from Sorghum, dear." Melody fluffed her feathers. "Bit warm after all that flapping. Why don't you try some of that smartweed, now." She looked toward the western horizon, which was already preparing an orange berth for the sun. "Better yet, we'll have a leisurely dinner, make ourselves comfy here for the night and leave fresh in the morning."

Melody gathered some succulent escargot and we ate our fill. Afterwards, while there was still light, she deftly constructed a rudimentary nest big enough for the two of us, a flimsy shell, but comforting—offering at least a sense of containment.

"I've never been this close to a swan," I said, snug against Melody's broad, white side, "except when I had a hold of Alexander's leg." I felt a twinge in my scars and forced my mind to cut off the memory of that.

"All in the past, now, love."

I'd never spent a night away from home. The smells were peculiar, more fishy. The evening sounds blended in an unfamiliar, edgy harmony, absent the pacifying quacks of retiring ducks, leaving voids of silence to be punctuated by sharp hoots and snarls from the woods a hundred yards inland. Most lacking was the presence of Mother, her evening story to look forward to. I tried to focus on what Sorghum might be like. There would be soft, cold rain every day. There would be a guard of some sort at the gate, a deputy of the Phoenix, barring otters from entry. Escargot would present themselves on demand. I imagined how I would feel when I met Madeline, Father and the rest of my lost family. I shivered with longing.

"Everything all right, dear?" Melody's warm breath puffed over my head.

"Yes," I sighed.

"Sure?"

"A bit homesick."

"What about a nice bedtime story—or perhaps a song. Which shall it be, dear?"

"Both would be nice," I grunted, reminding myself how webfoot empathy was one of the greatest of natural wonders.

Chapter 15

"Once, in passing," Melody began, her voice soothing and strong, "a mute swan and a tundra swan, their adolescent feathers newly white, fell in love at first glance. For months, they found ways to meet clandestinely. There was a kerfuffle, of course, when their secret was discovered. The families and flocks almost came to war over it."

"What were their names?" I asked, falling immediately into the story, my shoulder muscles, which ached from our long flight, relaxing. I swiveled my head to rest my bill across my back.

"Of course, dear. Serena was the pen, a lovely mute swan from a prominent Phoenix family, and the cob was Seth, whose father was a tundra Horus elder.

"Now, even though they'd been forbidden to see each other, their bond proved indivisible, and forced separation only strengthened it. For weeks the lovers pleaded and wept. At last, masquerading the inevitable as generosity, the families, with the counsel of their respective Phoenix and Horus priests, gave consent for marriage—with provisions."

"Provisions—like a catered wedding?"

"No, love, filial duties—with vows as to the raising of their cygnets."

"Oh."

"Specifically, Seth and Serena were sworn to provide religious instruction to all broods that they raised—Phoenixism to the cygnets that hatched as mutes and Horusanity to any that hatched as tundras."

"Sounds complicated."

"Quite. But it was meant strictly as a way to save face for the elders. No one imagined the pair could actually conceive offspring, being of two different species, as it were."

"Did they?"

"One must restrain oneself from pushing the narrator too far ahead, dear."

"Sorry—I do that with Mother, too."

"Actually, a month after the wedding, Serena laid a single egg. It caused quite the sensation. Everyone was beside themselves to know if it had been fertilized, whether it would hatch, and, if so, which parent the offspring would resemble—each flock harboring notions of being the dominant species. The priests made incantations against fertility—nevertheless tension grew."

I heard a splash near the shore and realized there was no ring of duck sentries around me to warn of otters. I shuddered and fluffed up my feathers.

"Not to worry about otters, dear," Melody reassured, reading my thoughts. "Are you feeling sleepy? We can finish this tomorrow."

"Not sleepy," I grunted. "What happened?"

"All right, then. Serena sat the egg for three weeks, Seth bringing her little delicacies, and all the time nosy birds of every kind crisscrossing past their nest. Finally, one sunny day toward noon, the shell cracked and out struggled a—what do you think?"

"Tundra!"

"No."

"Oh, a mute."

"Not that either, dear. Out came a two-headed cygnet. On one neck perched the tiny head of a tundra, on the other, a mute."

"Is that possible?"

"Of course it's possible, love. Have you never heard of Siamese swans? In any case, to properly enjoy a tale, one must suspend disbelief."

I tried to imagine this two-headed cygnet, to make it real—how it might entwine its spindly gray necks and look itself in the eye, tap its orange beaks together. I wondered if it thought separate thoughts and how it would make decisions—me finding it so difficult to make choices with only one head. In a few moments—my mind always a willing servant of fantasy—the cygnet became so real that I could see it quite plainly in front of me, smell its dry, feathery scent, and hear its twin throats piping in harmony.

"Ah, good, we're back in the story," Melody said.

"I'm trying to make it true," I said.

"All stories are true if we allow it, dear. It was certainly true for Serena and Seth, who cast their love upon their cygnet in infinite measure."

"Mother would have told me if there was ever a two-headed swan, though."

"There are millions of lakes in the world, dear. More places than anyone can know."

"What was his name? Or hers?"

"They called him Brace."

"Brace. Just one name?"

"You're reaching ahead again."

The sunset had long faded, leaving a crescent moon to hover above its own reflection in the silky lake. The upper sky was black and wild with stars, making me want to plunge into the future. "I'm here," I quacked.

"Jolly good, then," Melody declared, taking a deep breath, her port side pushing against me. "Basking in the security of his parent's love, Brace felt quite normal. Rather naturally, his two separate minds united under their single name and he was able to maintain a unity of purpose as he went about the business of growing up, learning to feed and fly like any young swan. When he spoke, it was always in a most charming duet.

"True to their covenant, Serena and Seth began to instruct Brace according to the principles of both Phoenixism and Horusanity. However, they found it impossible to direct their teaching separately to Brace's heads, since both were equally attentive. After a time, they simply alternated lessons, Phoenix one day, Horus the next, and hoped Brace would sort it out."

"Did he?" I interrupted.

"I was coming to that, love."

"Sorry again."

"As a matter of fact, Brace did find himself splitting up his religious legacies. Perhaps birds cannot contain two such basic, opposing ideas in one brain. Unfortunately, the liturgies of each religion lodged themselves, as it were, in the wrong heads—Phoenix in the tundra head and Horus in the mute.

"For the first time, Brace's unity began to break down. His two minds began to differ with each other about the merits of their beliefs. Discussion fell into argument. Shouting ensued. Within a fortnight, each of Brace's heads was demanding to be known by a different name."

"This is getting much more complicated than Mother's stories," I said.

"It's quite late," Melody said. "Why don't we finish tomorrow?"

"No, go on." But conflict always made my throat constrict. It felt as if a slug had lodged there.

"All right, a bit more, but another long day of flying awaits us tomorrow, dear," Melody cautioned. "Well," she resumed, fluffing her feathers, "you could hardly imagine the scandal of it and the disruption, and what a freak Brace became as a result—a freak not so much because he argued with himself—we all do that, even with one brain—but because for the first time he had become a threat to the status quo between the swan flocks. Prior to that, the mutes and tundras had considered him curious but benign and were even protective of him, chasing off mocking birds from time to time. But now, Brace's presence among them had become a danger to the social order. They began to conspire to rid themselves of him.

"In the meanwhile, because of the stress of internal discord and being snubbed by the other swans, poor Brace found himself in deep depression, barely able to function. Only the love of Serena and Seth kept him going, else he might have given up and committed suicide."

I felt a great gnaw of grief tear at my gut. If nothing else, ducks are visceral. "I can understand that," I mumbled, fatigue and sorrow now ganging up on me with sudden effect.

"Goodness, you're emoting at a dreadful rate. What is it, dear?"

"It's too sad."

"I'm feeling something a bit stronger than that."

"I want to hear the rest."

"Actually, I think we'll finish tomorrow, love. Now, I often sing myself a little lullaby before retiring. Would you mind?"

She crooned the sweetest sonata I'd ever heard, deep notes plunging and highs soaring like swallows, purging my sorrow and also my gut, so that I had to excuse myself from the nest for a moment.

"Melody, do you think a swan and a mallard could ever mate?" I asked, returning to my still-warm place.

"Hardly, dear."

Chapter 16

Brace had changed his name to Bracelet and we were cavorting—splashing together in a hot spring, piles of escargot heaped up on flat rocks. I awoke steaming hot. Accustomed to a bed of cold lake water, I was thermally unprepared to snuggle with Melody, whose torso gave off heat like a sun-baked boulder.

My feathers limp, I climbed out of our nest and wobbled down the gritty beach to the water's edge, the wet chill on my toes a bit of a shock, then bobbed up on an invigorating green swell. I paddled out, cooling down. Some gulls swooped low as dawn broke. The sun flared to life on the eastern horizon, upon which it seemed to rest for a time like an island ablaze, lighting or blocking the way home.

I thought about Brace and being at odds with oneself. One head was sufficient for that. Again, it always seemed to come down to choices. Who would teach Brace how to make them? I could hardly wait to hear the rest of the story.

I watched Melody, still asleep in the nest, her head tucked under a wing, the pose in which so many times I had seen her brother, Louis. So different were they—how impossible to judge temperament by appearance. "Know a bird's heart," Uncle Arthur always said. "Until then, you can't judge a rook from a plover." Generosity and courage poured from Melody's heart—so in contrast with Louis' cynical resignation. How does that happen, I wondered, in eggs of the same brood? Or perhaps it is really a matter of measure, of proportion in the mix. Being a bird, Melody would at times naturally know fear, and Louis had demonstrated at Father's funeral that he was capable of bravery. But what tips the balance so that one trait or the other stands above? Why was Troy so ambitious, Harold so pragmatic, I so timid? Why can't you choose which to be? That's the ultimate test, the choice that defies our will, I thought. Even the most willful bird can't make the most important decision—simply how to be. I guess you already are what you are. You just have to figure out how to be that.

When we reached Sorghum, the Phoenix would have the answers to these enigmas, I knew. Madeline and Father would already have been enlightened. They would be at peace. It seemed now so obvious what Pastor Jasper had said all along, that our lives here are only in preparation for the next life—a paradise, where the perfect Phoenix would govern all.

"Too much thinking so early in the morning," Melody called, rising from the nest, stretching her wings and reading my thoughts. "Breakfast before philosophy, I always say."

While we dined on morning slugs, Melody scanned westward, her dark eyes purposeful. "Weather looks favorable," she said. "Our objective will be to reach the general area where Sorghum is said to lie by early afternoon. When we get there, we'll reconnoiter and try to locate Louis, and then..."

"What about Madeline and Father?" I interrupted. "And the Phoenix?"

"Shan't forget them for a moment, dear." A sympathetic tone softened her voice. "But we are yet mere mortals, love, and we must be prepared for certain things to remain hidden, such as...."

"Hidden?" I blurted again, my newfound faith feeling entitled to all.

Melody drew a deep breath and lowered her head to my ear. "We must simply hope to find Louis alive," she whispered. "That is why we came. Of what awaits, we know nothing, love."

"Louis might be dead?" This possibility had never occurred to me. I had only considered that in Sorghum the dead might be found alive.

"One hopes for the best, dear."

I tried to cling to my vision of finding Madeline and Father—how our eyes would meet, the joy of recognition, ardent embraces, the majestic Phoenix hovering above in all his splendor, sending out arcs of blindingly golden light. But a chink of doubt had been opened. Questions I had pushed away like flotsam closed back in on me. Why would Clout take Louis to the Phoenix in a cage? If lost loved ones could be found in Sorghum, why weren't there regular excursions there? What was there that gave Troy nightmares? "Why can't we all just lead ordinary, peaceful lives, Melody—forever?" I asked, a tremor in my quack indicating deeper reconfigurations in progress.

"There's no life so ordinary or strange that it isn't eventually found by death, love. Not to fear, though. 'Live decently,' Papa used to say, 'and you will be ready for all that comes.'"

"But what about the afterlife?"

"We cannot know how the soul might be ensnared, dear, but we can imagine that it might be set free and what birds have imagined, no matter how fantastic, has always come to be." Melody stood, extending her wings, their great white span like a billowing cloud tethered to the earth. "Time to be off, then."

We fled the morning sun, which stained the eastern slopes of the peaks before us ocher, the dark cuts of crevices splaying out below the summits. In a short while, my sore muscles had limbered up. The regular twanging sound of Melody's ligaments set a rhythm and soon the repetitive motion became hypnotic, my ragged musings dissolving into blankness.

We were approaching the foothills, purple fingers of lakes filling many shadowed valleys. In the lee of the mountains, severe downdrafts pressed us lower, until we found a more buoyant layer of air just above the treetops, the scent of pine astringent. From this level, every scenic detail passed below in sharp relief—a doe watering, ripples spreading from the touch of her snout, the buck watchful, head turned, black eyes alert.

At the far shore of a longish lake, guarded by a pair of sentry pines, I saw the unmistakable silhouettes of floating ducks, six in all, and my heart leapt. Family! At the same time, Melody pulled up sharply. "Marcel! Climb!" she trumpeted. We were over water and I could see no obstacle, only our reflections separating in the glassy surface below. I aimed at the ducks, accelerating, sending quacks of joyous greeting ahead.

"Marcel! No!" Melody commanded as I prepared to land. I saw her reflection suddenly descend, scissoring in on mine, then felt the whack as she hit me full force, sending me crashing down into lake. Dazed, I looked up as she swung away in a perfect grace that suddenly went awry, as if the puff of smoke from the reeds near the perfectly composed ducks was a signal for her to go crazy, the discipline of the ducks holding fast despite a deafening clap of thunder from a sky as blue as a robin's egg.

Chapter 17

Few sights shock like that of a bloodstained swan. Before Melody struck the water, tumbling blurrily, bright red had already defiled the white perfection of her left wing. Paddling, flapping, I strained to reach her. "No! No! No!" I heard myself squawk. But space thickened and all time and propulsion bogged down. I could not close the distance between us. Another puff of smoke rose from the reeds and a second clap of thunder rang across the lake, this time sending invisible hornets fizzing overhead. In answer came Melody's defiant trumpet and my heart leapt with joy.

"Melody!" I squawked. "I'm coming!"

"Keep back, Marcel!" she warned, pain creasing her voice. "Head for that little island to the right—put it between you and them."

"I can't leave you!" I quacked, almost upon her.

"Go, now," she ordered. "Stay low. I'll be right behind."

As I veered right, my feet tucked up, belly skimming the water, a third report barked from the shore, slinging more hornets above, little jets spurting up on either side of me like minnows jumping.

In seconds, I was floating behind the island, gasping for breath. The mound of rocky earth, capped by spikes of coarse grass and a tiny blue spruce, was barely the length of Clout's canoe, but it stood tall enough to block the hunters' line of sight.

I peered around one side to see Melody paddling doggedly towards me, listing left, her wing now tinted pink, splayed out and dragging half-submerged. As I watched her approach, breasting the water in pain, her head erect, black-masked eyes resolute and dauntless, such a stab of remorse pierced me that I nearly passed out. With utter clarity I saw how one by one all whom I had adored fell victim to my bungling—Father, Madeline, Phoebe, Melody—all drawn into my trap, my circle of doom. I wished at that moment, prayed to the Phoenix, that Troy had left me to the otters. Through the eyes of my double, I saw myself back at Bloedel, watched as I ignored my brother, paddling on, to rightly relieve the world of a criminal, a habitual inflictor of suffering, a killer—myself.

But I did not need otters. There were hunters. I rose up on my wings, beating the water, ready to launch.

"Self-punishment can be so vain," I heard a voice say deep inside my head, echoing as if through the culvert pipe at Bloedel, "not to mention wasteful. Besides, no one is that important—and I need you."

I was not sure whose voice it was, but my wings collapsed and I flopped back into the lake. I began to sob, a low, cadenced grunting.

Then Melody was there, floating before me, and I could sense the pulse of her life beating strong. "Be still, love," she said. "Everything's all right."

I was trying to find a breath between sobs to beg Melody's forgiveness when dogs started to bark from the direction of the blind.

"Horrible, persistent beasts," she sighed, moving to the edge of the island to peer ashore. "Dreadful swimmers, though. They'll be in for a surprise if they try to come out here." She glanced at her left pinions, now rinsed almost white again, the wing slightly askew, not fully closed. "Forgiveness, you're thinking?" she said, turning to me. "Nonsense—I must take the blame for this, without question. I should never have taken us that low. You must have been frightened half to death, poor dear."

I moved to her, carefully adjusting the lie of a feather with my bill—as if, done with absolute precision, the wing would be restored to new. "You warned me, Melody. I've crippled you," I wept.

"All this self-pity is quite unbecoming, dear. I've already taken responsibility for this fowl-up. But I'm afraid you'll have to go on alone." There was a pinch in her voice—regret added to pain. "I might take a bit of time to heal up, mightn't I? More time than Louis would want to be kept waiting, I dare say."

"Alone?" The stun of the word silenced my blubbering.

"You'll be splendid, an eagle."

"I can't."

The dogs were yelping louder.

"Of course you can," she said, edging out again for a peek. "Two in the water, but they're circling."

"But who will take care of you?"

"Take care of me?" she laughed. "Why, the very same as always."

I looked at her, a regal and ancient courage in her countenance, as if she had long ago accepted her greatness as a necessary burden, noblesse oblige at large in the world, to be called upon by anyone, without apology, and offered more willingly than rain upon the dry earth.

She gazed back, patient, waiting.

"I really meant, 'Who will take care of *me*,'" I said.

"I know, dear. We must draw now upon forces greater than either of us."

"I couldn't leave you, Melody," I said.

"Rubbish. In a month, you'll have saved the day. You'll want to thank me for getting myself shot. Now, I'm going to have a bit of a nap. Keep an eye on those obnoxious dogs, love, if you wouldn't mind."

With that, her head sought privacy under her good wing, to mull the truth of her wounds, and it was as if she had already left me alone.

I looked around at the dark, pine-clothed foothills that loomed on either side, funneling the yelps of the dogs down the lake valley. Clouds were building into gray-bottomed white towers, cordoning off the sun, which in brief intervals poked through to shoot braids of glare across the breeze-knurled lake and to illuminate with a dull greenish glow the bass that slid through the seaweed beneath my feet.

A shiver of fear pimpled the flesh under my feathers. It seemed absurd to imagine that I would continue on by myself. Ducks traveled long distances only in flocks, and in twos and threes even on short hops to visit family—hardly ever alone. Bloedel—and Mother, Harold, Troy and the others—lay more than a day's journey to the southeast. But there was no going back now—certainly not without Melody. Somewhere northwest was Sorghum—how far, I knew not. And, even supposing I could find Sorghum, how would I recognize it? What would I do when I arrived? I wished I had never agreed to come at all. Melody could have found Louis herself—without getting shot. This wasn't a job for someone like me. Already my nerves were triggering another bowel response.

The dogs had taken up an unnerving howl, punctuated by yips and yaps, but for now they weren't coming closer. At the same time, I heard a familiar hoarse cry from the opposite shore and looked up to see a green heron gliding on fixed wings barely a foot above the surface of the lake. Seeing something, he pulled up to take a fishing position knee-deep near some cattails.

I stared at the heron, sinewy and ancient-looking, as if gauntness were the key to survival over epochs, that the lean would be best equipped to preserve ancient witnessing down through generations. I watched him take a few careful steps, as if feeling his way in the dark. Then his beak speared down, whipped up, clamped on a fish, his head and neck jerking to swallow.

Abruptly, he extended his broad wings, rose with a guttural croak, and with measured strokes, flapped east along the shoreline until disappearing around a point.

I turned to gaze at Melody, her pain quenched within her serenity, her majesty intact. The sun broke through the clouds again, gilding the scene with light, and with it the oddest sense of peace fell upon me, as if I were connected not only to her but also to the heron, all of birdkind, all of creation, the fish, the dogs, the stars.

The sensation welled up but a moment, then waned as a cloud shuttered off the sun, its shadow combing the glint out of the air. Yet one knows when one has been spoken to, even when the message is still encrypted. I felt the message as a hard capsule in my gizzard, something needing incubation, like an egg—not a familiar sensation for a drake, or a pleasant one, for that matter.

I wanted to follow the heron, to ask him how to dissolve the shell of my capsule, to unfold the message therein. But I couldn't leave Melody alone, and there were still the hunters and dogs.

The dogs had fallen silent. I drifted to the edge of the island and saw that they had gone ashore and were shaking water from their fur. The decoys had disappeared, leaving the vacant cove glassy and serene. A normalcy settled over the lake, the quietly efficient murmur of basic survival. Some frogs I hadn't noticed before were bleating insistently from the banks. Two yellow butterflies clung trembling to the scraggly little pine on our island and a fat beetle scuttled between blades of grass, drawing my attention to a pang of emptiness in my stomach. But my sense of connection persisted, reaching out to all frogs and butterflies and beetles. I wanted to give them something.

"One first has to be generous to oneself," I heard Melody say. "Otherwise, nothing can be given freely."

"Dear Melody," I quacked, pivoting to see her, my heart full.

Fresh, bright blood stained her wing. I dared not consider the extent of her injuries.

"You'll want to be underway soon, dear."

"Your wing…" I began.

"A fleabite," she interrupted, "but before you go, perhaps you could round up a leaf of skunk cabbage to pack under it, love—to take the nip out, you know—and maybe an escargot or two, if you should happen on some."

In an instant, I had launched to the shore, heedless of hunters or dogs. I tried to think only of Melody, pushing away the hunger that had begun to gnaw in my belly. This time, I would try not to gulp down any escargot before bringing them back to the island. Self-generosity and gluttony were not the same, it was clear—the patience to wait to share with Melody would be a respectful reward to myself, beyond pleasing her.

First, I found a skunk cabbage, its flat bouquet of fleshy, medicinal leaves spread out under a stand of birch. I tore off a leaf with my bill and hurried back to the island, and, as gingerly as I could, inserted the poultice between Melody's wing and body, my head abiding for a lingering, ecstatic moment in her most private, scented and secret warmth. I felt her wince in pain.

"Much better, dear," she said, a quaver in her voice. "Perhaps I'll follow you to the shore while you search out some dinner. No sense having to fetch food all the way out here, now that our hunter friends seem to have disbanded. Might scrape together a bit of a nest, as well…one never likes sleeping rough, really."

By climbing the bank, Melody was able to reach a safe-looking low shelf of shale with a view to all sides. Leaving her there, I cruised the banks, eyeing rocks and leaves for the familiar grayish spiral scroll of snail's shell. They were out in abundance that day—so many that before I could stop myself, I had snatched and swallowed an enormous and delectable specimen perched in the open on a flat stone. I was stricken immediately with guilt, imagining how it would have delighted Melody's palate. Then I countered to myself that she would have encouraged my self-generosity. There was still hardly any act I seemed able to undertake without endless echoes and reverberations of ethical second-guessing. I wondered how I would be able to venture on alone even an hour without becoming hopelessly entangled in self-doubt.

With that thought, the image of Brace appeared before me, his necks winding and unwinding in self-vexation like braided snakes. Here was my out. "How could I depart with his dilemma left hanging?" I would tell Melody. I would insist that I would have to spend the night here, so that she could finish the story.

But she would be in no condition to tell stories—I couldn't ask that. I decided I would hint and leave the decision to her—but a strong hint.

One by one, I retrieved our escargot, making a pile next to the nest Melody was constructing. It was a smaller nest, I observed, than the previous night's — an exact fit for her.

"Looks snug, Melody," I observed with disappointment.

"I wish you could stay, dear, but..." She hesitated and looked at me caringly. "But you mustn't lose time."

"I was hoping to hear the rest of the story of Brace."

"Brace? Oh, he turned out quite normal."

"Normal?"

"Of course, love—once he began to argue with himself, like all of us, he fit right in."

"But what happened to him?"

"Neither stories nor arguments are ever finished." She looked at the mound of escargot. "But I'm quite famished," she said, then turned a somber gaze upon the mountains. "Endings are illusions, Marcel."

"But all stories have endings," I said.

"Do they?"

"Mother's always did."

"Then why do we have to hear them over and over again, dear?"

There was a philosophical streak in trumpeter swans. At some point, their intelligence would bring me to where I felt as if the secret of all knowledge lay just beyond my comprehension, the boundary of my ignorance. "Maybe stories are like the Phoenix," I struggled, "and have to be reborn."

"*Like* the Phoenix? The story is the Phoenix, love."

I stared at her blankly. I had reached that point, my limit.

"No matter, dear," she said, moving toward me, lowering her head to mine. "You'll make your own story—that others will tell."

I shivered, whether from her hot breath or my inclusion in prophesy, I wasn't sure. "If I do, it will have an ending," I said.

"Undoubtedly, dear. But sometimes it's quite enough to just wonder what's beyond the horizon."

I left Melody there on the shore of the lake. I could hardly bear the pain of leaving her. As I ascended, spiraling up to view her snowy-white figure for what I secretly feared the last time, she sent me a cheery trumpet, full of encouragement, absent any sentimentality.

She had instructed me to follow a course north along the lower ridges of the mountains. If I found a road, I was to follow that, looking for a lake to shelter on for the night, but always alert for signs of humans, this being the time of year when they went berserk with their guns. Hunters or not, I always imagined the north to be a sinister region, everywhere a kind of dull, cold savagery, leaching away body heat. Yet there is a pull to the north that birds feel, which provides reference to the other cardinal points, and so one lives with an odd disparity—that knowing one's position depends on being constantly drawn to danger.

I flew into the turbulent rotor of the westerly wind that came over the mountains. High above floated the oddly smooth lenticular clouds that it was said only the Phoenix had ever reached. The violent agitation rocked me, my wings sawing, my body yawing and pitching.

I tried not to think about danger. I set to pumping my wings, a steady beat, letting my eyes relax focus. The features of the landscape dissolved into a blurry green. Every fifty beats—I had begun to count them—I let out a loud grunt. This felt good. *Forty-eight, forty-nine, fifty…Gruuunt!…One, two, three…*

I lost track of time. Suddenly, the turbulence ceased and the sun was sinking behind the mountains to my left, cloaking the foothills in shadowy contours and fetching back warmth from the air. The change brought the world back into focus. Numerous inky ponds passed below, filling in dips in the landscape, but so far no genuine lakes were in sight—ones with broad perimeters and open views that Melody said would suit me as lone sentry for myself. Leaving the safety of altitude was a frightening thought, but I did not want to be caught without options—aloft in the dark, exhausted, desperate to land.

Shortly, a narrow, unpaved road merged in from the east, bending north in the direction of my course and clinging to the base of the mountains. Heeding Melody's counsel, I tracked it.

Far ahead, just as I was resigning myself to a fitful night on one of the claustrophobic little ponds, a shaft of sunlight flamed through a cleft in the mountains, lighting up a distant facet of the terrain that I knew would be the surface of a lake. In great relief and expectation, I set to pumping my wings again.

In minutes, however, the golden shaft of light reddened and began to fade, the sun setting or no longer lining up with the cleft. The flare of the lake winked out and the landscape before me blended together once more like a rough, mottled hide. The deserted road below barely visible, I decided to follow it to the next pond and there call it quits. Soon, it would be pitch dark. Odd curtains of variegated, dancing blue and green light had begun to fill the sky.

My mind began to make random associations on its own. I thought I saw something heavy slouch across the ground, heading east. A tree reared up like a giant otter. A familiar cramp in my gizzard signaled oncoming panic and I fought against it. Strange, I thought, how I could want to kill myself one day and be frightened by shadows the next. Somehow, the anticipation of physical danger chases away the kind of fear that brings on thoughts of suicide—which for me was the fear of becoming an outcast, an albatross around the neck of our flock. Danger scaring away fear—that was a concept I would have to ask Louis about, and also how the albatross got such a reputation for onerousness.

But my fear went deeper than a reaction to a sense of danger—something to do with my feelings for Melody, an echo in myself of her vulnerability. Also, the story of Brace kept circling back. How would each of his brains respond to threat? Would each be aware of the other's fear?

East of the road, a dark blotch in the smudgy shadows marked another pond. Whatever it was, it would have to do for tonight, I decided. Banking right, I squared the blotch in my sights and began a descent, scanning all the time for signs of human life.

Behind me and to the right, the unmistakable croak of a heron made my heart bounce and I veered hard left.

"Late for a duck to be out," the heron said, pulling alongside with unlabored, even strokes of its wings.

"I've been looking for a lake to put in for the night," I informed him, leveling out, the roots of my neck feathers still tingling. The heron resembled the one I had seen that afternoon, but all herons are alike to me. Unlike other webfeet, they seem opaque to telepathy, impenetrable, a sense of lizard about them. Nevertheless, it was good to have company at that moment.

By then, the feeling of deep communion—the sense of weal—that had overcome me earlier seemed a dream. On the contrary, a troubling feeling of impending ruin was creeping in on me. "I thought I saw a lake farther on," I said, "but I lost sight of it when the sun went down. I was heading for that pond just below."

"Yes, sir, pretty late for a duck," the heron said. "Not for an owl, though."

It occurred to me that he might have some local knowledge. "You wouldn't happen to know of a nearby lake, would you?" I asked.

"Them owls stay up all night."

"Wouldn't have to be a big lake, sir," I persisted, "just with a little better margin of safety than a pond."

"Natural-born insomniacs, owls," the heron said. "Funny how the Almighty made some birds one way, and others he made different." He guffawed at this insight.

I laughed only in reflex. "Birds of a feather…" I began.

"Haw!" he interrupted. "'Margin of safety! You in politics?'"

I was letting down. The dark pond was coming up. There were no visible features on or around it.

"Looks mighty lonely down there," the heron said, suddenly serious. "I'll take you up to the lake, if you'd like."

"Thank you," I said. Pulling up, we banked north again, pumping wings to clear some swarthy pines.

"It's another hour, at least," the heron said as we leveled out. "Hope you got some owl in you. Haw!"

I was tired. The blue and green light pulsed in the sky, while the quarter moon stood fixed and bright, coaxing ghouls from the shadows below. I was glad not to be landing among them. Far ahead, twin pinpoints of other light began to blink on and off. "The eyes of the Phoenix!" my reckless imagination burst out, but a second later reason overruled—it would have to be a vehicle winding around obstructing hills. "Looks like a car," I said.

"Truck," the heron corrected.

"How do you know it's a truck?"

"Only vehicle ever comes this way. Every couple weeks. Big cage in the back, usually."

My fatigue evaporated. "Cage? My friend might be in there!" I quacked.

"Won't be no one in the cage," the heron said.

"Why not?"

"Nope, not on the return trip. He always leaves empty."

"Leaves where?"

"Up yonder."

"Up yonder where?"

"Cool your tail feathers, Mr. Margin O'Safety," the heron said in an irritated tone. "You'll see soon enough."

The truck's growl had crept upon the night. The fierce eyes of its headlights, haloes circling each, smeared a racing puddle of amber light on the road ahead. As the gleam and roar swept below, I pitched down, falling in behind the truck as it passed, seeking a shape, a box, a patch of white in the box. Too fast, the truck shot by, taillights receding, burning faintly through a plume of black dust that completely obscured my view. I wanted to follow but was torn between that impulse and the heron's conviction that the cage would be vacant. If I followed the truck, I knew I would not catch up with it until Bloedel. If the cage was empty, I would have wasted all effort and Melody's injury would have been in vain. If Louis was in the cage, he would be returned home, in any case, without my help.

The heron sent me a loud croak. "I told you it was empty. Haven't got all night. You coming or not? 'Course you are."

"I'm coming," I said, banking north again, excluding from my decision any consideration of what peril might lay ahead for me. I had had a justifiable chance—an excuse, anyway—to abort my mission and I had let it go. I felt a throb in the pit of my gizzard—as if my strange egg had shifted or grown—and tried to ignore it. It was only my aberrant imagination, or simple hunger, I told myself. To my knowledge, a drake had never laid anything.

"That's good," the heron said. "You just stay right here with me and you won't be getting into no trouble."

The disturbance of the truck gone, the landscape fell silent, like a great supine beast, returning to its meditation of the moon. The north exerted its baleful pull and we resumed our flight. I felt as if I was following the path of least resistance. The heron, I realized, seemed unduly dogmatic that I follow, as if the northern pull was somehow channeled through him.

After some while, I smelled water, a dank chill invading the air, a certain taint to it that I couldn't identify. "Must be getting close to the lake," I said.

"Won't be long," the heron said. "There's a cove some ducks find comfortable."

"Ducks?" I quacked. "There are ducks there?"

"You ever seen a lake with no ducks on it?"

I hadn't noticed a duck on any of the ponds I had passed, even when the light was good—or any other birds, come to think of it. "Mallards?" I asked.

"You a mallard?"

"Yes."

"Don't know my ducks real good. 'Seen one you seen them all,' my daddy used to say."

I bit my tongue. "How many ducks on the lake?" I asked.

"You do remind me of a feller came up this way last year, though," the heron said. "Had a whole flock behind him, lost as a mole in the sunshine. Except it was night, like now."

I lurched. "What was his name?" I demanded.

"Don't much like that tone," the heron said.

"Sorry!" I quacked. "That duck could be my brother!"

"Could? Can't tell yourselves apart, either, doesn't surprise me."

"Didn't he tell you his name?"

"Why should he? You didn't."

"Sorry, again. Mine is Marcel."

"Think he called himself, Tyrone."

"Troy!"

"Something like that. You sure you ain't him? Coming up on the south shore, now. You just stay right with me, Matlow."

Together, we dropped from dark to darker. I barely had time to recall Melody's remark about Troy being waylaid by a heron before I felt more than saw the water coming up and braked hard and late with my wings, feet plowing in deep—a squawky, splashy landing, but not on top of anyone, thank goodness. I listened for a second splash, which never came.

"G'night, Merlot," I heard the heron call, instead, already some distance away on his broad wings. "See you soon."

"Did you hear a splash?" I heard a duck say from across the lake.

"Go to sleep," another duck said.

My ears tuned to the murmuring of more mallards, the familiar night inflections of a duck cove. With each low quack, I felt a muscle release tension, a prickle of relief ripple down my spine. I heard a last croak of the heron in the distance. A long way off, an owl hooted. The smell lacing the night air was not acrid enough to keep me awake.

Chapter 18

When morning tugged me awake I found myself in the middle of a broad, turquoise lake, a cool eastern breeze fanning it into a fine rasp. Orange sunbeams arced from the eastern horizon, rusting the snowy tips of the western peaks and the undersides of some fair-weather clouds.

A distance away, snoozing in a cove, I saw a few dozen mallards, heads resting on their backs or tucked under wings—too many to be decoys and not suspiciously stiff. On the opposite shore squatted a large, gray, windowless building. All seemed tranquil enough, almost too quiet, no hint of danger, only that odd, unidentifiable odor—a bit fetid, like the matted-feather smell of the sick.

I hoped for the chance to thank the heron for escorting me here and to ask him how much farther on Sorghum lay. Of course, I could now ask directions of the mallards. But, for the moment, I wanted to rest a bit, to compose myself, to build up strength before pressing on. I tried not to fret about Melody, imagining instead how resourceful she would be, with plenty of food at wing while she healed.

The thought of food set off a twinge in my stomach, reminding me I had not eaten since yesterday. I flipped up my tail and ducked my head underwater to snatch up some reeds. Dull sunlight lit the shallow, yellowish gray bottom, which was smooth and completely devoid of growth. I scanned all around—nothing at all to eat down there. Puzzled, I came up for air.

Paddling twenty yards east, I plunged again. The bottom was as bald as concrete. I swam about for some time, head submerged, scouting for anything green.

Just as my lungs were about to burst, I bumped into a pair of mallard's legs, one with a bright band on it, and I lurched to the surface, gasping.

Before me bobbed a matronly duck.

She was flanked by a drake and another duck, the three of them ringed by half a dozen junior mallards. My random paddling must have steered me into their cove. No, the cove was yonder; they had swum to me.

"Hello!" I sputtered, squinting into the sun.

"It is him," the duck quacked to the drake. "Troy must be here, too." Her eyes locked onto mine. "Where is he, Marcel?"

"What?" I quacked. "How do you know me—and Troy?"

The other ducks stirred uneasily. Then I recognized her—it was Belle, Troy's mate. The drake was Nick, her brother, and the other duck his mate, Sarah. They all had curious auras, a bit sickly and hard to tune into, but it was they.

I stared at them, dumbfounded.

"Troy'd better *not* be here," Nick said, "if he knows what's good for him." Nick was large and was sending out menacing vibes.

"He's pretending he doesn't remember me," Belle said. "Has it been that long, Marcel?" She asked in a tone of mock reproach.

"I'm sorry, Belle!" I apologized. "I just didn't expect to see you here."

"My first brood is nine months, already," she went on, not seeming to hear. "Can you believe it? All grown up, now."

"What's left of them," Nick said.

"Don't be morbid, Nick," Belle said. "Or spiteful."

"What on earth are you doing on this lake?" I asked.

Belle pirouetted on the water, searching theatrically. "Now, where is that Troy hiding?"

Nick said, "Belle, you know Troy ain't coming back." He paddled up, abeam of me. I could feel his hostility like thorns. "Looks like the coward sent a surrogate, though."

"I'm trying to get to Sorghum—" I began, but no one seemed to be listening. "—to rescue Louis Wingstrong."

"Just give me a moment, Nick," Belle sighed. "You know I still care for Troy. I miss him and you'll have to live with that."

Nick fell silent and sullen.

Belle turned to me, abruptly all business. "To rescue who?"

"Clout took Louis away in his truck," I quacked, too obsessed with my mission to think about anything else. "I came with his sister, Melody, to find him. She was shot by some hunters, southeast of here. She said Clout was taking him to Sorghum." I looked around at the others. "Would you happen to know where that is?" They stared back. "I was hoping to find my dear departed mate, Madeline, and Father there, too, safe with the Phoenix. You see—"

"Where exactly is he?" Nick said.

"Louis? I just told you."

"Troy, you idiot."

"Oh, he's in Bloedel—recovering," I answered.

"Recovering!" Nick broke in. "I should have finished him off."

"Please, Nick," Belle said.

"Troy's all right," I said, "but Melody can't fly." I felt my throat knot.

Nick said, "And you left her—alone and wounded."

"No!" I sobbed. "She sent me on ahead."

"Just like Troy abandoned you, Belle," Nick said, contempt dripping from his bill. "Look at his brother, here—crocodile tears."

"I can fly and she couldn't—can't you see?" I quacked.

"Nick, let him talk," Belle said. A new light shone in her eyes. "He might be your chance."

"He's Troy's kin," Nick said. "I wouldn't trust him for a drink of water."

"A chance for what?" I said, trying to compose myself.

"We can't fly, either, Marcel," Belle said. "Nick needs—we need—your help."

"I don't need his help," Nick said.

"Can't fly? Why not?" I asked. They didn't appear injured.

"We're going to spread a spiritual revelation—a new truth," Sarah quacked. "A faith that will save all birdkind."

Nick gave her a cautionary glance.

"It's Nick's revelation," Belle said.

"I really can't get involved in anything new right now, Belle," I said, "what with Louis and…"

"Louis can wait, Marcel," Belle said. "Just listen a moment."

She related the story of their migration. After six days of hard travel, the flock had put down for the winter, on a lake set in a vast apple orchard. With an abundance of fermies, Troy had fallen into addiction. "He thought he'd found Sorghum," Belle said, "that he was in heaven."

"Sorghum?" I quacked, recalling Troy's reaction to the word.

"It was his joke, of course—ours, too, at first," Belle said, "but when it was time to leave, he didn't want to go. We had to force him."

Belle told how on the return flight to Bloedel, searching for another orchard, Troy had gotten them lost. They'd wandered up and down the peninsula until Nick challenged Troy's leadership. A terrific fight ensued between them. Troy got the worst of the brawl and flew away alone—which explained his condition the morning he showed up in Bloedel. Afterward, the flock had run across the heron, who'd guided them to this lake.

"We thought we'd just take temporary refuge here," Belle told me, "until we could get our bearings."

"It must be the same heron that brought me here!" I quacked.

"We call him the Smorgasbird," Sarah said. "The Great Provider." She looked across the lake at the gray building. "Praise the Smorgasbird, prophet of the great Phoenix, who provideth most bountifully."

Nick uttered a reverent grunt. "As told in the Bark, 'He guideth us to the Promised Lake, how blessed we are.'"

"Hail," intoned several of the other ducks, who had been eyeing me suspiciously.

"Then my brother doesn't know you're stranded here?" I said, trying to imagine what happened, beginning to feel Troy's shame. What would I say when I returned? How would he have explained to voters in Bloedel how he lost his flock?

"I should have got rid of him a lot sooner, the drunk," Nick said.

"Be grateful, Nick," Belle said. "You wouldn't have found your new faith here without Troy."

Nick glared at me. "We are not stranded," he quacked. "We are protected beneath the wings of the Smorgasbird."

"Just Nick and Sarah and I are all that's left of our original flock," Belle said. "These others are my offspring with Troy." She gathered them in with a motherly gaze. "The ones over there in the cove are Nick and Sarah's." She indicated them with a dip of her bill.

"What happened to the rest of the Bloedel ducks?" I asked. I had known all of them—many were cousins.

"Some kind of flu—swept through us like a forest fire." she said.

"And you…?"

"We survived," Belle said.

"More than survived," Sarah said, gazing at Belle with admiration. "Belle raised these by herself and she helped with mine." A shadow of sadness crossed her eyes. "And now with a new brood coming…"

"Now, Sarah, we helped one another," Belle interrupted, "spelling each other on the eggs, and all."

"A new brood," I said. "Why, congratulations, Sarah!"

Sarah looked away. "I pray the great Smorgasbird will reveal my sins," she said, a sad glance at Nick. "The reason for my rejection."

Nick sent her a sharp, dismissive glance, puffing up his feathers.

"Rejection?" I said.

"It's not Sarah's brood," Belle said.

"Oh, then whose?" I asked, looking at the younger ducks.

The question was greeted by silence and another hard glare from Nick.

"Well, it's nice to see you again," I said, finally, growing more edgy, "I will certainly tell all at Bloedel that I found you here, but I'd like to be on my way to find Louis—if you would just point me on my way."

Just then, a muffled screech came from the gray building.

"What was that?" I quacked.

"Maybe your friend, Louis—" Nick said.

Belle cut him off. "Leave him alone, Nick."

"—the same Louis that ran out on his wife, isn't it?" Nick went on, his glance enlisting the others for support. "Ran out on the whole reserve. Two peas in a pod, Louis and Troy—three peas with brother Marcel here."

Belle motioned her bill at the building. "Experiments, Marcel. It's kind of complicated."

"What kind of experiments?" The scars on my abdomen started to tighten. "And stop insulting my brother and my friend," I grunted at Nick, "and me."

Nick let out a vicious grunt that almost stopped my heart. "You bastard!"

Recoiling, I launched straight up, twisting in a tight, evasive loop. No one was following.

"You come back here, Marcel," Belle pleaded, looking up at me. "He's not going to hurt you."

I continued to circle. "I want to hear that from Nick."

"Nick, you need him," Belle said.

"All right," Nick said, "but I can't trust him. He's not of the faith."

"No," Belle said, "but maybe you can explain it to him." She lifted her eyes to me. "Nick believes all birds should sacrifice their wings to the Smorgasbird."

Another screech came from the building. It was hard to tell if it was the sound of something alive or some human's machine.

"I think I'll hang on to mine a bit longer, if he doesn't mind," I quacked, flapping hard to maintain a hover. "And what kind of experiments?" I repeated. Looking down, seeing all their heads tilted up, the younger mallards staring in amazement, a certain sense of superiority came over me—having the power of wings among the flightless. I had never before felt powerful, let alone confident, among other birds.

"He can fly!" one of Belle's brood quacked. "Like the Smorgasbird!"

"Shut up," Nick commanded.

I widened my orbit, for stability, and also as a demonstration—that if I chose, I could easily depart; I could leave them.

"And why can't you fly?" I demanded.

"Just come down—stay," Belle begged.

"Maybe," I said, not having to comply, gloating a bit. Rolling out toward the shore, where the building stood, I climbed higher, scanning for signs of humans. The bad smell worsened into acrid fumes and seemed to be coming from several spinning roof ventilators, which also emitted a low hum. A fat, corrugated metal pipe sloped from the building to the lake. A small boat was tied up near the pipe.

With the perspective of altitude, I could also see that a fence circled the lake. A high, wire-mesh screen, strands of it glinting in the sun, was set back from the shore, completely enclosing the building and the scrawny cottonwood and pine trees that fringed the lake. A gate in the fence, behind the building, blocked access to a road, possibly the one where I'd seen the truck the previous night. A thick cable, strung along the road on poles, terminated at a corner of the building. Peculiarly, not a single bird perched on the cable or on the edges of the roof.

Wary of approaching closer, I glided back to the cove and splashed in. Belle and the others tracked my descent with anxious eyes.

Belle paddled up, relief in her voice. "I thought you'd deserted us."

I glanced at Nick, who, with feathers flattened, looked smaller and less threatening. I puffed mine up. Something in even the meekest drake watches for a rival's dropped guard and presses for advantage. "I don't understand what's going on here," I said, trying a gruff tone. "What is this place?"

"It's Smorg," Nick answered.

"Smorg!" I gasped, my feathers collapsing. "Not Sorghum?"

"No, Smorg, lake of the Smorgasbird," Belle said.

"It can't be."

"Why not?" Sarah said. "It's as foretold in the Bark—"The Creator will return us to Paradise, the lake of Smorg.""

"I was hoping it was Sorghum, where the Phoenix lives… and Madeline and Father…and Louis, if he's dead, too, or still alive, I mean." I'd never felt so confused.

In a measured tone, Sarah said, "This is holy water, Marcel."

"Holy?" I squawked. "There's nothing alive in this lake. No fish, no plants, no tadpoles, nothing."

"Blasphemer," Nick said.

"What do you eat?" I asked.

Sarah looked across the lake at the gray building. "They bring it," she said.

"Bring what? Who?"

"Our sustenance," Belle said.

"A human female," Sarah said, "acting by the sacred edict of the Smorgasbird. Once a day. She takes it out in a boat and dumps it in the lake."

"Anoints the lake, Sarah," Nick said.

"Anoints," said Sarah.

"I just don't understand," I complained, my stomach contracting in hunger.

Belle swam closer. "Perhaps it's divine providence, Marcel, that you came here."

"What do you mean?"

"Tell me," she said, "what did you see up there?"

"I saw the building, a road, a boat, a big pipe," I listed, "and a fence."

"A fence," she repeated. "And what is the purpose of a fence?"

Mother taught me to wait politely after rhetorical questions, but I always forgot. "To block off?" I blurted.

Nick rolled his eyes and muttered something.

"We are privileged inmates, Marcel, surrendered to the holy Smorgasbird," Sarah said. "We are confined on this sacred lake for a great purpose."

I felt the strength of her conviction—deep, sincere, impervious to evidence and logic.

It did not seem possible for a mallard to be trapped on a lake but I considered the circumstances: it only required hobbled wings and a fence.

"How did you get trapped?" I asked.

"Not trapped, Marcel," Sarah said. "Surrendered."

"All right—surrendered." To me, the loss of one's wings was the definition of "trapped," no matter the words. An entire dimension was lost—the source of awe and liberty, what made birds transcendent.

"There'ssomethinginthefoodthatmakesyouabit—wobbly," Belle said. "One meal and you really can't launch."

"Then they come with a net," Sarah said.

"They take you to the building," Belle said. "A few are returned, banded, but most…"

"…a great honor," Sarah interjected, "to be considered so valuable."

"But trumpeter swans get honors, not ducks," I said.

"The last shall later be first," Nick grunted.

Winged or grounded, it had always seemed to me that there could be no greater earthly being than a trumpeter swan, the most perfect creature the Phoenix had ever created, so sublime and rare that humans held them captive. Now they were holding ducks captive. Ducks were no more rare than squirrels. "But why would humans want to keep ducks here?" I asked.

"We think it has something to do with us not being killed by that flu," Belle said.

"We are chosen," Nick said, his tail twitching aggressively.

"Maybe just immune," Belle said.

I looked at the building. "What's going on in there?"

Belle followed my gaze. "The woman comes to take one of our offspring every month." Her voice faltered. "Six, so far, of my brood."

"Praise the Smorgasbird," Nick said, "who provideth us food."

"Food for all," Sarah said, "in exchange for a few ducklings—ones that might die, anyway, if they turned out not to be immune in the next outbreak."

"*Might* die?" I quacked.

Sarah looked away.

"They keep us at about forty," Belle said.

"It's all horrible," I grunted.

"No, no, it's the sacred cycle," Sarah objected. "We lay, we sit, the ducklings hatch, some are blessed for holy sacrifice." She began to cry. "It's so beautiful."

"Sarah," Belle said, looking toward the cove, "why don't you and Nick take your ducklings for their swim before our meal comes? They're looking a bit restless over there."

Some of the ducklings in the cove were thrashing about, pecking at each other. Nick spun about and quacked, "Hey, stop that!" He and Sarah paddled off. "Don't you be meddling in this, Marcel," Nick called back.

"Frankly, Nick has it too good here," Belle said to me in a kind of desperate, conspiratorial quack. "Phoenix knows the times I've wanted to give up, but Sarah says we must have hope, and she's right, so I go on, waiting for a miracle."

"Miracle?"

"I try to follow the Bark," Belle said, "but you don't imagine certain things will ever apply to you—the Twenty-second Presentment, for one."

"What about it?"

"Sarah stopped laying, for some reason. The next brood is mine and Nick's. He's my brother, as you know. He said the Bark commands us—the Twenty-second Presentment."

"What?" I stammered. I recalled that the Twenty-second Presentment says, "A drake shall give shelter to his brother's mate if he maketh her a widow."

"Don't judge him, Marcel—or me," Belle said. "Survival changes things."

I wanted to think fairly of Nick and to avoid trying to interpret the words, "shelter" and "brother," which I had always thought meant "protect" and "comrade." Mother said the Bark was often ambiguous and could mean whatever you wanted it to—or needed it to, like now, when you had to put survival ahead of shame. Whatever else, though, the Presentment didn't say, "A drake shall commit incest with his sister." But I didn't have the heart at that moment to say this to Belle.

Belle said, "Listen, we have to talk quickly, Marcel, before my brother returns." She glanced at the cove, where the ducklings had fallen in behind Nick and Sarah for their swim. "You can fly," Belle said. "You are my miracle. You'll teach my next brood how to fly, help them escape this hell." Her gaze was anguished, candid—under her pale eyebrows, the amber stripes in her eyes were like crystal filaments. "Won't you, Marcel?"

Louis said that the only miracle is the way the universe fits together so perfectly, how everything around us meshes. He said we long for new tricks that will save us from paying our dues—tricks that *we* imagine to be miracles—but that is merely the vanity of our wills, to save us from the process of natural law. He said that those who persist into adulthood in their faith in miracles, despite mounting evidence to the contrary, end up as fools.

"Or saints," Belle added. "You will help us, won't you, Marcel?" she repeated.

I hadn't realized my thoughts were that transparent.

"I'll convince Nick that the new ducklings will spread forth faith in the Smorgasbird, if we can just get them outside the fence—to preach, I'll say."

"I'm kind of in shock, here, Belle, confused, anyway."

"We don't have time for shock or confusion or melodrama, Marcel."

"I'll have to think about it, Belle," I said. "I can't just abandon Louis."

"You can't abandon me, Marcel," Belle said. "You're not like Troy, are you?"

"But I made a promise to Louis, and to Melody," I quacked, stung, and at the same time realizing I hadn't promised anything to anyone, just gone along.

"Shush, here comes Nick," Belle whispered.

"I believe we might have had trumpeter for lunch yesterday." Nick grunted a sardonic laugh, having overheard mention of Louis. "Very tasty."

"Don't be crude, Nick," Belle said. "Or maybe you'd like to dissolve our, um, arrangement." She paddled over to stare him in the eye, until a dip of his head showed contrition, then she returned to me. "I laid twenty-five days ago, Marcel. That leaves three more days to hatch, another eight weeks before they could fly. Then you'd take over—in secret, of course. The humans can't know you're here." She paddled back to Nick. "Marcel's agreed to help us send out my coming brood—of

Smorgasbird missionaries—dear. Just like you've always hoped. He'll teach them to fly. They're going to reach the far corners of the world, carrying the truth."

"What?" Nick grunted. He gave me a contemptuous stare. "This heathen? And how would they be able to fly, anyway?"

"Come with me, dear brother, I'm going to tell you all about it."

As they departed, leaving me with Sarah, I felt my stomach twinge, whether from hunger or apprehension, I wasn't sure. I tried to ponder what Belle was proposing, weighing it against my allegiance to Louis and Melody, but my head began to spin, making my stomach feel worse. Suddenly, my attention was drawn to the opposite shore, where a human was boarding the boat.

"Dinner," Sarah said, a rueful fringe to her aura as she watched Belle and Nick sail away.

"At last," I said. "I'm starved."

"You can't eat this food," Sarah said. "Don't ever forget that, Marcel, ever. If you're going to teach the brood to fly, you'll have to find something to eat on the other side of the fence—for you and the ducklings, when they come."

The putt-putt of the boat started up and I watched as a stiff wind blew the oily, blue smoke of its motor out ahead of it. The smoke mixed nastily with the odor from the building. Shortly, as the boat crept towards us, I could make out that the human seemed to have the same color head fur as the one I had seen with Clout in Bloedel.

"Get out of here, Marcel," Sarah quacked. "Find yourself some dinner and come back in an hour."

I launched. Circling, I watched the boat make its way steadily toward the waiting mallards, a scene of startling desperation. I knew then that the eggs Belle had laid and the feeling of an egg within me were somehow connected, a conjoined brood that would hatch my destiny.

Chapter 19

The local ponds furnished a lavish menu of reeds, escargot and slugs. As I gorged myself—the food spiced with no small measure of guilt—I fretted what I would do now about Louis. I could not have imagined I would stumble on a place like this, instead of the splendor and peace of Sorghum I'd expected—the reunion with loved ones and the merciful Phoenix on high, blessing all. My hopes were now all but drowned, and the inescapable logic of Louis's fate stared me in the face: the road ended at the gray building. I pondered whether I could find a way, or even muster the courage, to peek inside.

The thought sent shivers down my back feathers. Belle's scheme, for the present, was a welcome diversion—a different sort of challenge, if not less daunting. Locating and hauling rations for a full brood, numbering ten to twelve ducklings, seemed beyond the wherewithal of a single mallard—all day, every day, for the two months it would take their flight feathers to grow in. What if I got caught? Tainted? Sick? One bite of the human's food by the hatchlings or me and all would be for naught. Moreover, my next molt was due to begin only two weeks after the earliest the brood would be capable of flight, setting a limit of fourteen training days.

Nor had I considered the implications of this scheme. What might happen should the ducklings succeed in escaping? Where would they go? What skullduggery might Nick have vested in them? Questions about the future only made my head spin.

On a more practical level, I decided to test my logistical capacity. I found I could carry only two medium escargot at a time in my bill—possibly I could work it up to three. If all twelve of the brood survived, that meant, at peak growth, appetites for six escargot or slugs per duckling per day—a total of seventy-two. Toting seventy-two mollusks, at three per trip, would require twenty-four trips per day (Phoenix only knew how long it would take just to find that many). At a rate of, say, ten minutes per trip, that would take six hours of flying per day, not including extra time to ferry in reeds and vegetation necessary for a balanced diet. Added to the challenge of airlifting food would be the drain on my time and energy for flying lessons.

The plan did not seem feasible. One mallard has only a finite amount of time and energy. Belle's zeal to liberate an entire brood from Smorg was inspiring but unrealistic. Ducklings were ravenous. I couldn't feed them all. If I stayed to help, she would have to make selections, draw straws. And even supposing, at great toil, I did succeed in helping a few to escape, what would that prove? Was it too harsh of me to observe that it wasn't as if Belle's flock was being tortured, or that they were the only ducks left on earth?

This brought me back to my original objective. I could not deny I had made an unspoken pledge to Melody. I had come to rescue my friend and her brother, Louis—abducted and, well, real. These ducklings, unhatched, did not yet exist, nor was my brother, Troy, even the father, while Nick, the veritable—and incestuous—father despised me. Why would I risk putting my own freedom and safety on the line for him? If I were smart, I would move away from the lake, to a pond—farther away from the smell and the chance of getting snared by a human—while I worked on a plan to find Louis.

Conversely, the mallards here were in sorry straits and I did feel a family allegiance to Belle. She was, after all, a duck. It is not a canard that charity begins at home.

I decided I would tell Belle that she would have to select one, maybe two, from the brood. They would be the chosen escapees. The rest would have to resign themselves to life in Smorg—the only life they would have known, in any case.

"I can't favor some above the others, Marcel," Belle replied when I told her. "No, you'll have to find someone to help you."

"Who would I find?" I quacked.

"Someone," Belle said.

There could be other ducks on surrounding ponds, I supposed, although I hadn't seen any. Not one bird had flown over Smorg since I'd arrived.

I'd brought back two escargot, one each for Belle and Sarah, who shook their heads. "You can bring us something after the hatching," Belle said. "Until then, build up your strength—eat them yourself."

I looked at Nick and gobbled down the escargot.

"The guilt must be killing him," Nick said to Belle, "but I'm thinking there's something suspicious about this whole deal."

"You won't say that after you've spread Sorgism to all bird-kind, Nick," Belle answered. "And you, Marcel, will be known far and wide as a saint."

"Or a fool," I thought to myself.

Launching again, I decided to climb high, to think, and to look for any ducks that might be nesting on ponds within a twenty-minute radius of the lake.

Abruptly, the eyes of my double opened, and I viewed myself rising freely from the entrapment of the lake, at liberty to continue in flight for as long as I cared, at my sole discretion—back to the southeast, if I wished, to Melody, and from there, home to my family in Bloedel.

It is only when I saw myself through the eyes of my double, I realized, that my fateful decisions were made—fateful, insofar as I became aware of the struggles in my heart. Then came a detachment, a breathing space—from erroneously presumed and conflicting obligations. Whether I continued to search for Louis, stayed to help Belle, returned to Bloedel, or set off on my own to parts unknown—my time was my own, to do with as I alone decided. Decisions made with this awareness, not simply in blind, emotional reaction, were in some way fiercely binding.

I marveled at how my double would suddenly incarnate—always perched above my right wing—when it was time to choose, and how he revealed all the nooks and crannies of my fears. I had never talked with anyone about my double, or asked if they had one. I wondered if the Phoenix had a double to consult with in making decisions—probably not, since a double seemed to be a sort of parasite of the weak, albeit a benevolent one, and the Phoenix was strong, although with so many birds praying to him for help, he must wish he had one as an assistant.

I decided that Louis would have to wait.

Among the scores of ponds ringing the lake, I saw not a single duck. A few eagles circled high in the azure updraft above the mountains. Several miles from the gray building, some blackbirds perched on the wire along the road. Once, from a distance, I thought I saw the heron sweep above the lake, but when I looked again there was nothing. What would be of interest to a heron on a fishless lake? He seemed to be husbanding the flock, luring ducks there, to be trapped by the humans. But that did not make sense.

I doubted there would be any other ducks in the area. The smell would keep them away. Dropping lower, I scanned ponds for nests. Shortly, I passed over a nice round pool, set in a glade in a forest of tall pines. I descended smartly, splashing in hard to evacuate anything below the surface that might have an interest in my feet.

It was a tranquil, primeval setting, the pond ringed by tall trees all around in a tight green cylinder, a small circle of sky visible at the top—a little too tight, I thought, the banks already cramping me in. Nevertheless, it was a gourmand's delight, a bountiful colony of escargot on the banks, three on a stone, sometimes, and a growth of tender reeds just below the water's surface, so thick they might have been farmed. In a few moments, however, I was overwhelmed by the urge to spread my wings, to escape. My heart began to pound. A bird simply cannot stand being closed in.

Hearing a small rustle in the woods, I exploded away as if it had been a shot, spiraling up to where I could breathe in the open sky above the treetops.

In the distance shone the lake. It was easy to appreciate its beauty from here, so remote from the misery of the ducks trapped there. Again, my double materialized above my right wing, his gaze panning before me, as if I were elevated beyond where eagles flew.

I saw the confining pond I had just fled, the stifling bondage of Belle's flock on the lake, Louis possibly being tortured in the gray building, Melody stranded far from home, Bloedel and its devastating swan wars, trouble and pain everywhere. And here soared I, apart, above, safe and aloof, like some self-appointed Phoenix.

A lonely, decisive grunt escaped my throat.

Chapter 20

"You could start to stockpile, now," Belle said matter-of-factly, as if she'd known all along I would agree to help. "Some baby slugs, for example. We'll keep them in the shade, near the nest. No one will touch them." She looked at Nick. "Will they."

"How will you keep the new brood from feeding on the human's food like everyone else?" I asked.

Belle looked at me. "Just do your job, Marcel, and I'll do mine."

With three days to go before the hatch, I busied myself gouging out a slug repository in the damp earth with my feet and bill. I sealed the bottom with a layer of small, flat stones. Then I flew off to fetch a billfull of slugs from a nearby pond. Belle instructed two of her children to guard the hole and to flick back any maverick slugs that made it up to the rim. I was skeptical—the temptation for the guards to nibble would be irresistible, I thought, greater than I could have withstood. But Belle was confident in their discipline, and she proved right. There was also a risk that heavy rain could wash away the result of days of harvesting. Nevertheless, I persevered and the weather stayed dry. Every hour, the guards spritzed water in the hole to keep their charges moist. After about thirty trips to the pond, an inch depth of sleek, baby slugs were slipping over each other in the repository, the perky antennae and palatable, gray sheen of their bodies indicating robust health.

On the evening before the final morning, time seemed to cling to the moon, dragging it back as it tried to cross the stars. You could feel the flock's sleepless energy riffling through the damp night air, intensifying the ubiquitous blue and green light that rippled overhead. At last, a vagrant ray of dawn sliced through a gap in the trees to shine on the nest, where Belle had taken over the sitting from Sarah. The flock went still, floating in the cove, watching, waiting.

In a while, you could see that Belle felt something. She murmured a quack. She wiggled, then edged aside. The first egg had pipped. Shortly, more fine cracks appeared in it. An hour later, the shell fell to pieces and the tiniest, pale amber chick staggered out from its encasement. A great quacking cheer erupted in the cove. By evening, eight more ducklings were tottering about the nest among fragments of shell, bumping like dandelion heads against each other, their peeps barely audible.

The following morning, another egg hatched, but the other two remained smooth and solid, as still as green stones.

Belle looked happy. "Your ten pupils, teacher," she beamed at me. They huddled against her.

"Ten diners, for now," I corrected. "But congratulations."

"I forgot how nice it is."

"What about the other two?" Nick asked.

She looked away. "Wait 'til tomorrow, Nick. Then…whatever you like." She turned to me. "He wasn't like this before, Marcel. It's the food. We have to get the ducklings out."

I felt my scars tighten. I walked away and slipped into the lake.

The time for planning was over. Now there were actual, teeny bills pecking at the air. My purpose in life was set for the next two months. My shoulders tensed. Glancing back at Belle, I thought of my Madeline—denied her brood, her chance to lay, to sit, to nurse. Sadness gripped my heart. I felt something shift in my belly, a pressure. "Is my strange egg ready, too?" I thought, but it was just gas.

Time to get to work—I launched, the birth scene receding beneath me.

I had already marked the best ponds for escargot, slugs, reeds, berries, shoots and seeds and had worked out a daily airlift schematic. Having allowed for twelve mouths to feed, I had found after some initial practice runs that I could scarcely complete my rounds before sunset. A reduction by two mouths was in fact a relief.

New ducklings need sugar for the first few days. With at least a two-day supply of slugs already laid in for protein, I focused on tender shoots and ripe berries. Not far from Pond 11—I had numbered my route—grew a rampant stand of blackberry vines, laden with fruit, it being the high season. Knowing my fragile gizzard would pay later, I still couldn't help gobbling down a few billfulls. I wished I were able to carry food with my feet, like a hawk—it would be a lot easier to restrain myself.

By late afternoon, I had heaped a pile of berries and another of tender shoots from Pond 8 alongside the slug repository, as well as some dry seed and fine sand for grit. The ravenous ducklings tore into the piles. The guards blocked them from the slugs, which they wouldn't be able to digest for a few more days. By dusk, they had consumed my day's work.

Belle gave me a nuzzle. "Better get some rest, busy beaver."

Nick sent me a baleful stare as I trudged the few yards to the water and paddled out to my sleeping-place. I was exhausted. My muscles ached. As I dropped into sleep, the sky above the mountains still burned where the sun had vanished. A hush fell over the lake.

A terrific screeching and squawking shattered the silence. My senses jumped awake. The sky was pale, the trees black silhouettes, giving no clue whether it was evening or morning. A heavy shape lumbered overhead, climbing steeply, wings whapping.

"My babies!" Belle wailed from shore.

I catapulted myself to the nest. In the dim light, chicks were squeaking and darting about in frenzy, Belle trying to scoop them back with her wings. Behind me, other ducks were clambering out of the lake.

"What happened?" I squawked.

"The Smorgasbird!" I heard Sarah quack behind me.

"Oh, Sarah, Sarah," Belle cried, "my babies—I've lost them, he got them."

"That filthy savage!" Sarah quacked, rushing to Belle, shielding her with one wing, sweeping with the other to help gather in the ducklings. "He knows, he waits—it's not your fault, dear."

"Sarah!" Nick barked.

"I'm sorry, Nick, I can't help it," Sarah answered. "It's too barbaric—how many of mine he took."

"You'll see them in the next world," Nick said. "You know that. On earth, you must submit to the divine."

Sarah hung her head. "I know."

"These didn't even have names, yet, Sarah," Belle cried. "How will the Phoenix even know them?"

I looked up, knowing what had happened. The sky was empty. I looked at the nest, counting eight chicks.

"The Phoenix numbers us all, Belle," Sarah said.

"The damn heron numbers us all," Belle spit, "with subtraction."

"No, no, dear," Sarah consoled. "Don't say that."

"I must give the others names this very morning."

Clearly, it had happened before. I began to see the heron's system. He would watch the nest and know when a brood was coming. He could pick off the chicks at his convenience in complete safety, no one able to pursue him.

"Why didn't you tell me?" I demanded. "I could have stopped him."

"He's always waited until at least the third night," Sarah answered. "I was going to tell you then, afraid you would leave us."

"I'm going to sleep by the nest," I said, not knowing if I dared, "starting now."

"No, you're not," Nick said. "You can't interfere with our sacred duty—I'll see to that."

Threats from the sky and on earth—there would be no place secure for me.

Chapter 21

Belle woke me even before dawn, before anyone else was up, the sky pale and luminous, like the interior of a vast eggshell.

"Come with me," she said.

I followed her to the nest. The ducklings clumped together, their tiny bills pinching air. As Belle settled in, they burrowed into her down.

"By these names, I declare my children forever bound to you, Great Phoenix, and to the Bark." she said. "And the Smorgasbird be damned."

The first she named after me ("He shall follow you."), the next two after Sarah ("May this one not suffer.") and herself ("May she find peace."), the fourth after Nick ("I have to."). That left four more, two ducks and two drakes—as best we could tell. Against my protests, she left their appellations to me. "They're all in your care and you should have a say in what to call them," she said.

Right away, I decided upon Madeline and Basil—names I would have wanted for my own offspring, had my dear mate lived, had she laid.

"Be careful, Marcel," Belle said, "not all may survive. You don't want to risk doubling your loss."

I considered this. "It's all right," I said. "They'd get to meet their namesakes in Sorghum, if that is the name of heaven." It was a problem to name anyone or anything—the words never seemed to fit exactly the qualities they were supposed to signify, at least not until a long time later, when you got used to them.

That left a duck and a drake. "Phoebe," I decided.

"One more," Belle said.

I couldn't think of another. "I'll have to wait for inspiration," I said.

"No, we can't leave any nameless," Belle said. "Without names, evil powers can snatch us away—like the heron."

"Belle, is there anything to this Smorgism stuff?" I asked.

"No," she said. "And anything that eats my babies doesn't deserve the dignity of a name."

"What about abandoning your babies?"

She thought for a moment. "Only the Phoenix can judge."

I looked at her. "Troy, then."

Belle said. "I knew you would."

Before beginning my daily foraging routine, I pieced together a small nest for myself a few yards from the nursery—from where, at twilight, I would make it a point to launch, grunting and flapping hard in a tight, defensive radius above the little ones, to make my presence known. The heron stayed away.

First thing in the morning, I would call each chick by name, although at that age you really had to concentrate to tell them apart, their auras being weak and undifferentiated, mingled like patches of sunlight filtered through tree leaves.

The ducklings were voracious. Over the next few days, I worked my bill to the bone. The weather turned wet, a blessing, soothing my overheated muscles as I made one trip after another to gather provisions. During one deluge, I was afraid the slug repository would fill up and its contents overflow or drown, but I managed to cut a sluice into the pit, which I could open or close for drainage by inserting a stone.

Nick had begun at once to immerse the chicks in the eschatology of his vision of a new religious order. At sundown, he would wait until they had nestled close to Belle and, in a monotone grunt, expound the principles of what he called, "Smorgism." Of course, the brood couldn't understand a word; nevertheless, their father persisted, knowing how words take root in infant brains, later to leaf into orthodoxy, adopted uncritically.

And perhaps he would be proven right. Most birds in Bloedel—including me—clung to the beliefs they were raised with, rather than risk being shunned.

Nick claimed that the truths of all previous prophets and demigods—especially those of the Phoenix and Horus—had been distilled into Smorgism, and that the Smorgasbird's singular holiness now would be a beacon for all birdkind. He said that he, Nick, was the sole anointed priest of the Smorgasbird, committed to carrying its edicts to the far corners of the world.

"Those that came before were great, but the Smorgasbird is greater," Nick intoned to the chicks. "His power is invested in me. I am his obedient servant and you will be my messengers."

"Let them rest, Nick," Belle would plead after an hour or so of this.

"They must learn," Nick would snap back, "so that they can teach." Then he would resume his catechism. "Those who refuse to abide the purity of the ordinations of the Smorgasbird will perish in everlasting ice. . ."

Eventually, his voice would tire and peace would fall upon the cove as he waddled away toward the lifeless water. Nick slept on the lake with Sarah and the others. I would have only a few moments alone with Belle before fatigue overtook me. One night, after Nick had gone, I said, "Belle, the chicks will end up brainwashed before they leave."

"I know," she said.

"Can't you do something?"

"Just get them out."

"By the time they're ready to fly, they won't be able to think for themselves," I said.

"You'll have to help them with that."

"You know I don't have time. You're giving in to Nick's nonsense."

"Nick's my brother, Marcel," she said. "It hasn't been easy for him, losing the use of his wings—on account of Troy, must I remind you? But he's kept us alive all this time."

"He'd kill me if he had half a chance."

"You can fly. You're a threat to his pride and his authority here. He uses that frightful heron as his proxy."

Gazing up at the jumbled stars, I pondered this and sighed.

"Don't wait for Nick to change," Belle said. "Just get on with it."

Piecemeal, over the weeks, we exchanged the events of our lives since the migration. Only a mallard can fully share the zeitgeist of another mallard. I told her about father's death, and Madeline's.

"How awful," Belle said. "You must miss them terribly."

I looked at her. "Yes, I do."

"And Madeline, did she have a brood?"

I shook my head.

"Poor dear."

The ducklings grew, patterns in their feathers darkening, the drakes brighter than the ducks, all their appetites becoming insatiable, until the rations I had piled up began to dwindle and I felt I could never catch up. How to gather more food became an obsession, blotting out any other thoughts.

I learned what a luxury it was to find time to reflect. In a state of perpetual exhaustion, I plodded to my nest only after the last useful ray of light had faded, to sink instantly into a dead sleep. There was hardly time to say good morning to Belle. I saw Sarah only from on high, a brown smudge among smudges on the lake, as she busied herself with her broods.

One day, I realized I had slipped behind schedule. The ducklings had consumed all reserves and by the end of the day, I was still short. Night fell. It was a new moon and the landscape was opaque, black as tar, too dark to fly or forage.

The brood began an incessant, desperate begging, experiencing for the first time the pang of unsatisfied need. It was a heart-rending sound. The younger ducks out on the lake picked it up and began to quack in sympathy. I was beside myself with anxiety, fearing the worst—that I could never catch up, that the ducklings would die or be forced to eat the toxic food the human brought. The din went on for hours and, despite my complete enervation, I could not doze off.

Then I heard a shuffling near the nest and felt Nick's presence. I heard Belle squawk and the ducklings thrown into greater commotion.

"No!" Belle cried.

"He can't feed them, I'll feed them!" Nick blared.

I charged towards the sound, stepping into the slug pit and wrenching my foot. I winced in pain, stumbling forward straight into the nest, bumping bodies, brushing against the frantic chicks.

Nick squawked and I felt his hard bill drive down and glance off my right wing. I stabbed back, catching him somewhere in his underbelly, the flesh soft. He grunted in pain.

"Stop!" Belle screeched. "Stop or I'll kill them all myself."

I froze, breathing hard in the pitch dark. Nick went still. Around us, the brood carried on with their wailing, driven only by hunger.

"They'll tire themselves out soon," Belle said. "Get out of here."

"I'll catch up tomorrow, Belle," I panted. "I promise."

"You'd better," Nick grunted.

"Both of you, get out of here," Belle said, crying.

As soon as there was light to see, ignoring my bruised wing and the ache in my foot, I made a start. I altered my route, lopping twenty minutes off the entire circuit, thus adding time for an additional delivery. I increased the proportion of mollusk in the diet, hoping to quell the brood's hunger with richer food, needing fewer trips.

By late afternoon, I felt I was noticeably ahead of my previous efforts and my hopes rose. Landing with a billful of slugs, I saw that there were only four ducklings waiting with Belle.

"Where are the others?" I asked, grateful to rest for a moment.

Belle looked at me.

"The heron!" I squawked. "Or Nick! I'll kill them both!"

"No," Belle said. "Kill me."

"What?"

"Nick was right," she said. "You can't feed them all and teach them to fly. You knew that at the beginning—and so did I, really."

I looked at the four milling about our legs, gobbling up the reeds I had dropped. They were Troy, Nick, Madeline and Marcel.

"Belle…" I said, tears welling up.

"Even four may be too many," she interrupted.

"And the others?"

She peered out at the lake. "They'll be fine, just like us."

Following her eyes, I wondered what was the definition of "fine." Were flightless mallards on a poisoned lake "fine?" Was Melody "fine?" Louis? Troy? Myself? Was "fine" merely to be one step ahead of death? Maybe "fine" was to be in Sorghum, in Heaven—one step after death.

Chapter 22

With only half the mouths to feed, the wave of relief I felt could not rinse away my guilt at sending four more innocent ducks to lifetime confinement on the lake. They would languish there with the others for as many years as it took to die, lugging about the dead weight of their wings, digesting the toxic slop the humans dumped.

"It's not your fault," Belle said. "I'm sad, too, but we have to move on—we have to be practical."

Belle refused to allow the ducklings she had sent out to the lake to fraternize with the remaining "flyers," as she called them. "It would only breed jealousy and resentment," she said, "especially once the flyers learn to launch. Besides, Nick won't allow it."

"Why not?"

"He tells the ducklings that only gods can fly."

"What does he tell them about me when I'm not here?"

"They think you're a god, of course."

"Me?" I blinked in disbelief—I, the paragon of impotence, a god.

"An evil god, anyway," Belle said. "Nick says he has power over you, that he prayed to the heron to bring you here—as his devil slave."

Strange, I thought, how when someone starts to lose control, their stories get more and more bizarre and convoluted. It was alarming to be thought of as a devil, someone with the intent and power to cause harm. Did the ducklings believe this? I glanced down, feeling my always-hungry cadets nudging my legs. "What will he say when these little goslings start launching?" I asked Belle.

"He'll think of something."

"Do they know they will fly?"

"Not yet."

I wasn't so certain. You tried to supervise your telepathy but thoughts leaked out. Thinking is by nature secretive and few birds can keep a secret, or want to.

As Belle had intended, fewer trips for food gave me more time to plan my flight lessons. Harking back to my own youth in Bloedel, I recalled the dismay and dread I had felt watching other ducklings, brood by brood, take to their wings. When my turn came, it had seemed impossible. I loved just trailing behind Mother, solid ground under my feet or my belly buoyant in the water. I would have been quite content to be an amphibian. The prospect of cruising around in the sky, tempting the force of gravity, nothing but thin air separating my soft parts from the rocks below, made my gizzard churn. But Mother and Father had prodded me on.

Now, I would be provider, teacher — prodder.

With my molt due in two weeks, I would have to complete all training by then. After that, until my feathers grew back, I would be rendered flightless and would need to camp outside the confines of the lake. The flyers would have to be able to clear the top of the fence, giving them ongoing access to healthy food without my help.

Flickering in the back of my mind was the disturbing image of me stranded on some pond, featherless, watching the ducklings flap off by themselves to parts unknown. I would have to ask Belle about that.

Molting is something mallards usually take in stride. Twice a year, your feathers fall out like fluff from split-open milkweed—refreshing in a nude sort of way, despite leaving you earthbound, comical and vulnerable. A drake's bright coloration vanished along with his plumage, molting males adorned for a time in the same drab camouflage as the ducks — not all that protective, really, since no halfway intelligent predator is easily duped. So you laid low while your pinions regrew, fattening on escargot, repeating old stories, passing the time of day with friends and family. Molting was a time for rest and rejuvenation.

Now, however, my molt loomed up like the otter in my nightmare. I felt the same sense of imminent doom — of not having time to launch before gnashing teeth snatched me.

The next morning, after breakfast, I gathered the flyers around me. They were beautiful mallards with bright, heroic auras. Despite my worries, my heart swelled with pride. Soon, I hoped, would theirs.

"Troy, little Nick, Madeline and Marcel," I announced, anticipating their joy, "in two weeks, you will know what it is to fly."

They shuffled uneasily. Little Troy uttered a nervous giggle. "The Smorgasbird wouldn't let us do that," he quacked.

"We'd be devils, like you," little Marcel added, more assertive than I ever was.

Nick was devious and the devious seek out the impressionable, sowing suspicion of all but themselves. Here was my own namesake, already distrustful of me. I looked at Belle.

"I'll fetch him," she said.

I watched Belle paddle out into the cove. It was a calm, humid day. Oily-looking ripples fanned out as she cut the smooth water. The sun was trying to burn through mist but succeeded only in thickening the ever-present stench from the building. The ducklings here hadn't a clue about what was pure and natural. My resolve to help the flyers escape quickened.

In a few minutes, Nick swaggered ashore, Belle behind. "Why didn't you tell me you were going to get started?" he grunted at me.

"If you want your little messengers to fly, you'd better straighten out their heads soon," I said, thinking aloud how my molt would soon begin.

"Marcel…" Belle started to say, alarm in her voice.

"Molt?" Nick broke in.

Too late, I realized I had not guarded my telepathy.

The bat was out of the bag. "You don't think I'd go through a molt on this side of the fence, do you?" I thought I was getting better at the sarcasm of rhetorical questions but I didn't like the way Nick's eyes narrowed while he considered this.

Belle was blinking nervously. "You want to get our missionaries on their way as soon as possible, don't you, Nick?" she said. "To spread the word of the Smorgasbird."

Nick closed his eyes in inscrutable silence. Then he opened them. He turned to the ducklings. "Praise the Smorgasbird," he quacked.

"Praise," they repeated.

"You will fly," he commanded.

"We will fly," they echoed.

Nick looked at me. "Teach them," he grunted, his tail swinging as he tramped away.

"You shouldn't have let slip about your molt, Marcel," Belle said in a sharp tone I hadn't heard before.

"Why not?" I shot back defensively, because she was right.

She sighed. "I don't know…makes you vulnerable, somehow. I know I always feel a bit ashamed without feathers on."

I shuddered. The obedience of the ducklings to Nick was frightening, like the legions of swans commanded by Cyrus and Alexander—opaque to reason, blind extensions of their leaders' wills. It was more than conceivable that Nick would be scheming to turn the flyers to diabolical ends.

They were now eight weeks old. I lined them up for inspection. Psychologically, they were still juveniles, of course—compliant more than dedicated, easily distracted, but I was sure that would change once they had tasted flight. Their feathers had grown in well, to the stage of maturity needed to generate enough lifting force and for control in the air. The notched juvenal tail feathers were in place. Their extended wings appeared symmetrical, flexible and strong.

I proceeded with lesson number one. "Making a beeline from point A to point B is not all that difficult," I lectured. "Most of the work is in mastering our take-offs and landings." I had decided to start with a water launch rather than a ground take-off—mainly because the former was more difficult, with more initial drag to overcome, and also because they would need that skill once outside the fence. Despite some misgivings about the toxic water, Belle had already taken them, at my insistence, for their first swim.

Demonstrating a simple launch, I illustrated how to drive the wings down hard with the shoulder muscles, then relax momentarily before the next muscular pump. "Conserve energy," I advised. "Let an imaginary helper on each side lift your wingtips after each downstroke." At the same time, I explained how one needs to get the abdomen off the water as soon as possible, minimizing friction and the attendant drain on power. Dragging the toes, however, was permissible for a short distance, while building up speed in preparation for a climb.

Little Nick was the first to volunteer. His first try, which had me clamping my bill lest a quack of hilarity escape, looked more like a drunken ecstatic display than an attempt to fly. The other ducklings were less inclined to stifle their mirth, and so by the end of the two-hour lesson, all were in better spirits than I could have hoped for.

Then it was time for me to resume gathering their provisions.

We worked every morning. By the end of the first week—after about fifteen hours of demonstrations and practice—their progress was gratifying. While you couldn't call it flying, Madeline, Nick and Marcel could flap several yards, toes dragging, belly clear of the water—but not little Troy. He preferred instead to paddle along at a modest rate, his wings fanning slowly like a heron, his chest parting the water like a little dory. With only a week remaining, I was concerned that he might not be able to catch up with the others.

"I need some help with Troy," I said to Belle that evening. Nick had finished his proselytizing and had gone out to the cove.

"I noticed."

"What do you suggest?"

"I'll take care of it."

I looked at her. "Please don't. He'll make it."

But in the morning, only Madeline, Nick and Marcel greeted me.

"Belle…" I said, my heart aching for Troy, knowing she'd been right about names.

She stopped me. "I told you it's not your fault, Marcel. I'll just have to make sure Nick doesn't pick on him. But no time to talk, now," she quacked, "we must hide the others."

"Hide them?"

My eyes followed hers to the cove. There sat the boat, low in the water, two human figures weighing it almost to the gunwales. It was Clout!—and the woman.

"They're counting," Belle said. "They'll know there was a new brood and come looking for the nest."

We hustled the flyers away, into a clump of juniper near the fence. Belle crowded them into a crevice at the roots, scratching dead leaves and twigs over them. I collected some more debris and in a few minutes, except for some slight movement of the camouflage as the ducklings settled in, you couldn't detect the hiding place.

"Not a word," Belle ordered them. "Play dead." She looked at me. "I'll see you later."

I launched, then angled high above the boat, the faces of the humans tilted up at me in the pale mist. Clout, at the stern, started up the motor and the boat moved off toward the low bank, where our nests were. I circled to watch. The boat beached and Clout got out, helped the woman step to shore and pulled the prow up on some pebbles. They walked straight to Belle's nest and began to pace about, heads down. Clout bent to pick something up and threw it away. Then he walked toward the juniper and my stomach knotted.

Belle in the meantime had made her way to the opposite side of her nest and suddenly started up a great ruckus of quacking. She hopped and squawked until Clout and the woman reversed tracks to investigate. When they reached her, Belle abruptly stretched out one wing and began to hop in a circle as if demented. Clout tried to pick her up but she pecked fiercely at his arm and he dropped her. I was suddenly afraid her diversion had gone too far and that Clout would catch her in a net and take her away.

I dived down like a hawk, swooping so close to Clout's head that my wingtip creased his ear, all the time squawking at the top of my lungs. I hadn't felt so stirred to action since I tried to protect Troy from Alexander at Father's funeral. It felt quite good.

Clout grabbed the woman by the hand and ran back to the boat. As they chugged away, I made another pass — this time not so close, discretion being the better part of raptor, as Father would say. Clout tried to bat me away, the boat rocking, taking on water. The woman screeched and stood up and the boat capsized and turned turtle, the motor sticking up and screaming as loud as the woman until it sputtered out. The lake was shallow and the humans waded waist-deep back to the beach, then trudged the shoreline to the building, the woman punching at Clout.

"Can we speed up the lessons?" Belle asked later, the three remaining flyers out on the water practicing. "Clout will be back for another look and we can't hide them for long."

"Maybe another session in the afternoons," I said, "if I can gather enough food." They were eating more, now, burning up extra energy. I felt tired, unsure.

All the while, I had been thinking about Louis. Last I'd seen him, he was in Clout's truck. Now, here was Clout. I looked across at the impenetrable-looking building, opposing waves of hope and despair agitating in my stomach. I had failed Louis, and now stood to fail Belle. I longed to be back in Bloedel, in our family duck cove, surrounded by the familiar sights and sounds of life—above all, the bracing smell of fresh ocean-pine air.

"Marcel?" Belle called. "I'm depending on you."

A little encouragement goes a long way.

With two lessons per day, the flyers made swift progress. It was just as well. On the tenth morning, I awoke to find fluff in my nest.

"I must have miscalculated," I said to Belle.

"How much time do you have?" she asked.

"Not more than a day. You know how the flight pinions fall out first."

"I'll have to tell Nick he'd better finish up his part," Belle said. "If the flyers leave before he gives permission, there'll be no living with him."

I realized then that Belle would have to live under Nick's tyranny no matter the outcome of the escape.

"Maybe," Belle said. I must have been broadcasting again. "But Nick had our survival at heart. At least at first. We depended on him to keep going. You can't imagine what it's like to lose the use of wings, the taste of food. We wanted to give up."

I thought about Louis, who did give up. "What happened to Nick?"

"He tasted a different kind of food—power. His ambitions were frustrated all his life, Marcel, ignored at Bloedel, shoved aside by Troy on the migration. Here, he was dictator."

By afternoon, it was apparent to me that all three flyers would be able to clear the fence. I felt a nervous excitement. But we had been so fixated on this one goal that Belle and I had never talked about what would come next. Where would the flyers fly? Would they simply nest on a local pond? Migrate south? Or, Phoenix forbid, return to Smorg?

"We'll leave in the morning," I said to Belle. "I'll have to put down right away to molt. I don't know where the flyers will go after that. You'll have to talk to them."

"Just let them go," she said.

"Let them go?"

"We don't want to control what's free." She gave me a nuzzle. "I'm going to miss you, Marcel."

"But I'll be just outside the fence — at least until my feathers grow back."

Her eyes brimmed over with tears. "Don't you ever come back here."

I gazed out at the lake, dismal and spoiled, set in untold acres of natural beauty. Here, Belle would remain. All the affection I had locked away when Madeline was killed suddenly burst forth, squeezing from my heart an almost unbearable pain. I blubbered like a chick. "I don't really want to be free, Belle. I need someone to do things for."

"Charity begins at home, Marcel," Belle said, her voice hard and resigned. "Free the ducklings. Then set yourself free, too."

Chapter 23

A ll night, I listened to a soft rain caress the cove, the murmur of ducks rippling in, an utter darkness surrendered
to gentle rhythms, but my pulse drummed with anticipation
and worry. It was as if sound were time itself, the hours wearing on as long as something maintained a beat.

Eventually, the rain ceased, the ducks slept. By and by, a flat,
silver light began to steal across the lake. Dawn approached,
and with it, the pain, once again, of separation. Bonds were
made, only to be broken, no pact spared.

I stood and shook my tail—more loose feathers. There was
no time to lose. I felt starved, but this morning breakfast for
the flyers and me lay on the other side of the fence. I heard a
rustle and knew that Belle was awake. Nick grunted from the
cove and I watched him head for shore, Sarah in his wake, and
mount the beach in his swaggering gait. The silhouette of a
heron glided past—what did he suspect?

Nick's quack shattered the peace. "Gather here, my children!" Clamped in his bill was a drake quill, a long, chest-
nut-colored pinion with speculum markings. With a shock, I
glanced at my wings—it wasn't mine.

The flyers advanced, Belle coming to stand by me. "Ready?"
she said.

"As much as I'll ever be," I said.

Nick stood before the flyers. "In the name of the Smorgas-bird, I anoint you," he declared. "Nick...Marcel...Madeline." With each name, he stroked a duckling with the feather. "Open your bills," he commanded. He touched the feather to each of their tongues. "You shall carry the seed of the Smorg wherever you go."

Nick turned to me. "Are they ready?" he grunted.

I nodded.

"Whose quill is that?" Belle asked.

"It's from one of the ducks that died of the flu," Sarah said. "To spread to the unsaved."

"What?" I quacked.

"Shut up!" Nick grunted at her, then to the ducklings, "Fly, my children, fly!" And then he was upon me, tearing at my feath-ers. "Now you're going to see what it's like to be crippled!"

I staggered back, upended, Nick's vicious bill ripping at my wings. I caught a glimpse of ducks against sky, heard the beating wings of a launch. I tried to right myself, to position for take-off, but Nick barged into me, bowling me over again, all the time plucking at my plumage, bits of down flying off into the air.

Then Belle was in the fray, hoarse with fury. "I'll kill you, Nick, I'll kill you!" she squawked, and I felt Nick's attack abruptly cease as he dealt with her attack. Reeling back, I drove my wings down hard for a launch, but veered sideways into Sarah, who was quacking in terror. Realizing I must have lost some flight feathers, I pumped again, this time favoring the left side, which seemed to lack normal lifting force. Unable to gain altitude, I flopped toward the lake in a low, wobbly trajec-tory, my toes leaving scratches in the ground, then grooves in the sandy beach, then trails in the water.

Behind me, I heard an enraged quack as Nick broke free and a chase began. I lost control again, splashing into the lake as he gained on me. Shaking off water, I surged forward on my wings once again, the eastern sky now ablaze with the rising sun. Every time I tried to pitch higher, I would involuntarily bank left, my wingtip catching the water, ditching me. Nick was closing the gap with a steady, hard paddle, his grunts ferocious. He was almost upon me. Once more, I pumped my wings, leaning to the good side, my toes dragging. "I've got you," Nick squawked.

I pumped hard, once, twice, trying to keep straight and level, felt myself veer, recovered, pumped, my feet like stones, shoulder muscles burning, giving out.

And then I was airborne. I don't know how.

I climbed twenty feet, cleared the fence, dodged some pines, heard Nick curse, Belle cheer. Skimming low, I raced to the nearest pond, hoping I could make it. I didn't want to be stuck in the wild underbrush of the forest.

The blue pond hove into view between trees and as I dived toward it, I felt my right wing skew as a pinion pulled loose and I spun downward, the earth rushing to meet me.

Chapter 24

Iplunged down into the cushy branches of a hawthorn, spiky, but not nearly so unfortunate, I noted with relief, as would have been the adjacent lichen-encrusted granite boulder — or Nick's clutches, for that matter. Sliding to the earth with a thump, I checked myself over — no harm done, as far as I could tell, only some missing plumage which had caught on the hawthorn spines.

I looked around. A few hundred yards of dense undergrowth lay between me and the pond. It would be a long slog on foot.

As I trudged ahead, a steady drizzle pattered on my back. Tangles of honeysuckle snared my legs, making progress slow and exhausting. Walking is an absurd method of locomotion. I stopped often to rest. I found nothing edible along the way, save a couple of bitter-tasting beetles, which I spat out. Never mind, there would be ample food soon.

By the time I broke into the clearing, it was past noon. The rain had ceased and a blue hole torn in the overcast framed the sun, the dazzling reflection of which burned in the pond. Briefly acknowledging the beauty of the scene, I directed my attention to finding breakfast, a hollow belly being the absolute monarch of body and mind. Having often exploited this pond for the ducklings' food, I knew it to be a cornucopia, its banks a source of delectable escargot and slugs, with tender reeds prospering in the shallows and sweet blackberry on the west side. I would be able to last out my molt here in comfort—physiologically speaking, anyway, barring predators, and providing I could endure the isolation. It would be only temporary isolation, though. As soon as I my new flight feathers grew in, I would set off to—actually, I had no idea where I would set off to. And right now, I was too hungry to think.

I gorged on mollusks, stuffed my gullet with reeds, topped off on berries, settled into the sun-warmed grass on the south bank and fell straight into a luxurious, dreamless sleep.

When I awoke, night had fallen. Crickets were clicking, a sound I hadn't heard since leaving Melody. A frog honked. With no nest built, I slipped instinctively into the liquid shadows of the water. I wasn't used to waking alone in the night. For a moment, I forgot where I was. Just above the tree line, a faintly marbled half moon had risen like a gigantic fragment of hatched eggshell. Its light silvered the edges of drifting black clouds and drew a luminous vapor from the pond, as if some new sky was birthing.

I felt an odd expectation, as if I had been summoned to witness arcane events. In the stillness, I could hear the steady thump of my heart in my breast. The night seemed then to cloak all but the audible expressions of the universe, the crickets to mark celestial time, frogs to divulge the boundaries of space—and my heart to signify my presence as a witness.

An owl hooted, sending a shiver down my spine—another presence. I inhaled deeply. The night air tasted fresh, though the relentless stench of Smorg had numbed my olfactory system. I quacked to the owl—no response. In any case, I wouldn't have known what to say to an owl.

I had never passed a night without close company. A lone duck quickly becomes anxious. We are dreadfully addicted to the nearness of others. Already, I missed Belle and the ducklings. I could feel my heart begin to long for Mother, for all my family, for Melody and Louis, for Madeline. I might even have felt the absence of Nick, there being some remnant of every acute relationship to cling to. I didn't know how I would last a complete molt in solitude. I understood even less how Louis would want to isolate himself in response to his loss, like having a tryst with pain.

I wondered if I would ever find Louis. What a trap I had fallen into on the lake. I had trusted the heron. I trusted too much. You see someone in genuine need, like Belle, and your natural impulse to help gets appropriated into someone else's calculated scheme—Nick's, in this case. Everything had gotten so complicated. As for the flyers, I dared not contemplate their destiny—or my role in it. If they had indeed been tainted with the flu, I could be responsible for wiping out whole populations. At the very least, they could spread Nick's pernicious religion. I could have inflicted mortal and spiritual plagues on all birdkind. I could only hope that contact with sane birds would restore their natural sanity. Where lay my responsibility in all this? For now, for the future.

My head throbbed. It was too much to think about. I tried to go back to sleep, but my mind continued to grind like a human's log chipper, pieces flying everywhere. I craved the company of another warm webfoot.

My fretting didn't derail the crickets, which went on with their doleful ticking, slowly ratcheting the moon across the heavens. Implacable, the throaty frogs staked out territory.

I prayed that whatever deity was responsible for the growth of feathers was on the job. I knew I couldn't spend much longer spinning in my thoughts, ruminating over past mistakes, imagining what might or might not lie ahead, what was true, what was false, what was fair and unfair. It would drive me insane. I would end up like Louis—a recluse with nothing but words for company.

As usual, my gut signaled its opinion. It suggested compensation—the gastronomical paradise of the pond. I envisioned a sumptuous breakfast. That would be good. I fell back to sleep.

Dawn broke and I ate my fill. Then I went to work. I designed a comfy nest — lavish, actually. My down was coming out in billfulls so I lined the rough twigs of the interior, first with soft ferns and then with a layer of my fluff. Unconsciously, I had allowed room in the construction for Belle, but then I thought guiltily about Madeline and reduced the size to a tidy single.

I took my time, pausing frequently to rest and snack. Without the pressure to feed the ducklings, dining was relaxed and pleasurable, the reeds delicate to the palate, the escargot most savory, the berries piquant.

By noon, the crickets had waked to serenade and I stopped work and settled down in some warm grass for a nap. As I dozed off, a cloud of gnats was stirring the autumn-scented air. Water striders dimpled the surface of the pond. It seemed as if I were back home in Bloedel.

I completed the nest just before sundown. I had reserved my longest molted quill as a final touch — stuck upright in the twigs at a jaunty angle. I celebrated with an extravagant supper and snuggled into my first-class accommodation. The sky had turned a festive violet. My stomach full, the concerns of yesterday retreated into the distance. This was more like it. To be happy in life, perhaps one had only to make up one's mind to rejoice in its bounty.

And yet I had a premonition of something bad to come. It was not an unfamiliar feeling, the same that had in the past led me into trouble — that I deserved to be punished for some misconduct, for misfortune I could have prevented, or simply for being an inadequate duck in general. I was bound by shame and my fate sloped downward.

The color of the western sky deepened and the last glow drained into the earth. Below ground, according to one of Mother's stories, the moon would be preparing to rise, transmuting the purple spikes of the sun's radiance into its own bone-white luster. In the meantime, frogs resumed their demarcations. Crickets continued to clock eternity. I felt the secure pressure of my wings against the walls of the nest and found myself imagining Madeline on one side and Belle on the other. As if in derision, the owl hooted—this was weakness, it seemed to chide: be a drake, stand strong.

Morning came and another opulent day passed. The autumn weather brought rain one hour, sun the next. I foraged for escargot when it showered, snoozed when the sky cleared. I kept my belly full. But at night my heart was empty—yearning and anxious. A full stomach was no substitute for companionship. As soon as night fell, I would settle into my nest and begin to count cricket chirps, hoping to drop off to sleep before the hard ache of loneliness set in. In the coming weeks, the sun would set earlier and earlier. I didn't look forward to more darkness but there was nothing to do about it. My molt wouldn't be complete for at least a month.

Happily, my new plumage was already growing in, the drab colors of first molt—the eclipse, as it's called. I would have to wait for the second molt to restore my drake's bright hues, but that was fine—there were no ducks to attract, anyway, and my only desire was for flight feathers—to fly, to fly.

I imagined my launch, the strenuous pumping of wings, the thick drag of water finally overcome, breaching the spare and limitless sky—a magical tunnel to anywhere. A thrill went down my spine—the freedom!

I began to contemplate my first destination: I would press on to Sorghum to find Louis. No, Sorghum was turning out to be mythological, and, to be honest, without Melody at lead point I would be too frightened now of exploring the unknown. Better, I would hop back over to Smorg Lake, to investigate what was in the building—possibly Louis had been there all along. And I missed Belle terribly. No, Nick and the heron would try to finish me off.

Better still, I would return to Bloedel to reunite with family. Melody and I would make new plans to locate Louis. By then, she would have healed and we could venture out together, even to confront the heron. No, first I should backtrack to the lake where I left her, in case she hadn't yet recovered. And by now Troy might have led Bloedel into turmoil, if not into civil war—Phoenix against Horus, swan against swan. He might need my help. Father would have wanted me to help him. I shivered at that prospect. Maybe Louis was right. One has to stay outside, uninvolved, maintain one's distance, keep a clear head, detach. When it came time to leave this pond, cold, reasoned self-interest would direct my next move. For that I would need my double. I wondered how to conjure him. He only came unbidden.

Loneliness was hollowing out a nest in my heart. To count the days, I gnawed grooves in the bark of a low hanging cottonwood limb. On the fifteenth evening, settled in my nest, I began to cough. I thought I had felt a tickle in my chest after lunch but attributed it to the damp air. I hadn't really been ill since a duckling. But by nightfall, I felt hot, my tongue went dry, my eyes burned. My head started to pound like a woodpecker and I retired to my nest. What was the incubation period of the flu? Had the toxins of the lake infused into my body?

Shortly, a fever commenced to rage in earnest. Thinking to cool off, I tried to make my way to the pond, but the world began to spin. After two steps, I stumbled and fell. I retched up dinner. I struggled back to my nest, burrowing in. Congestion was taking root in my lungs and I began to wheeze. It was all worsening too quickly. I felt a pang of fear, my flesh crawled. Was I going to die? That's the way it happened with the flu. One minute you were fine, the next your lungs filled up with phlegm and you were dead.

This couldn't be happening. I wasn't ready to die—no, not yet, not this time, not after I'd finally stood up to life. I hadn't said goodbye to anyone. I hadn't found Louis. No one knew where I was. I felt as if I were drowning. A chill racked my body and my bones shook and scraped like winter tree branches. Raw, lonely agony knotted in my gut and I cried out, "Mother!"

The trees began to shift and tilt, sway and moan. High above, the blue and green lights flashed and flared. The full moon turned a sickly yellow, casting the caustic disk of its reflection upon the pond. A rushing black cloud blotted out the sky. Yet the Moon's image remained floating on the water. Then it began to sink beneath the surface, whereupon I saw the pond begin to roil and steam. Green fire surged in its depths. Above me, pairs of eyes burned from jagged tree limbs. A ropy incandescent spiral twisted in the sky like a great serpent, white forks of lightning spiking out, and thunder pounded my nest. The owl screamed in rage and the stench of Smorg Lake poured in from the woods like a suffocating fog.

Suddenly, the pond erupted. Out of a geyser of boiling foam rose two great beasts — an otter, drooling bloody saliva, its coat slick with slime, eyes crimson; and with it, entwined, somehow, a grotesque heron, its puckered, featherless skin stretched over bony wings like great skeins of spider webs, the point of its beak dripping amber venom. The creatures ascended, towered above me, writhing, while I squawked in terror, pinned in my nest. Then I was clamped upon them, riding their backs, whipped one way and the other, then thrown, flung high, spinning, tumbling.

The fumes sent blades of pain ripping through my chest. I could not suck in air. I was lost, I was drowning. I sped to death.

"Great Phoenix!" I cried, "Save me!"

Then came a calm in all creation, time frozen, a slab of silence as must reign on the floor of the sea. My breath stopped. My feathers went flat. The silence began to drum, as if the heartbeats of earth and sky had joined. I seemed to emerge from my body as a separate mallard and without any need to flap I floated up to the treetops, where I could look down upon my carcass, which was tipped over on its side.

This peculiar juxtaposition struck me as quite natural and proper and it suddenly seemed as if I had become my double; no, it was clear — I knew and understood without the slightest doubt that I *was* my double.

182   *Donald J. Berk*

I felt a tide of confused dismay. In the dirt below lay my dead body, pathetic in its ravaged ordinariness, one dim, open eye staring up at me. There would be no requiem, nor even acknowledgement that this duck, this former I, once occupied a place in the living world. Yet here was I, attendant to my own corpse. The dismay converted to panic. There was some mistake. I wanted to merge myself back into myself.

And then came the rippling notes, a song in the purest voice, sweeter than the refrain of any trumpeter swan, enrapturing all of time and space that ever were and ever would be, delighting the universe within and without, and then the song emitted a great crystal of light, which in the distance flamed brighter than the sun and I glided toward the light like a moth and I knew the light would incinerate my flesh and I would be new and immortal like the Phoenix himself. And from the light came a voice: "You must return for now, Marcel. You will not be afraid."

No! I only wanted the light, the combusting, symphonic, perfecting, cleaving light.

A day, three days, a week—how long, I don't really know. Tongue stuck dry in my throat, eyes caked, too drained even to muster a cough, it took me half the morning to stumble pebble by twig to the pond for a sip. The few cold drops down my gullet stung as if I had swallowed nettles.

It was another five sunrises before I considered a nibble of reed. My lungs ached. I wheezed. I shivered in my nest all night. But none of that seemed to matter. Hadn't I, Marcel, been sent back from the dead — re-hatched and transfigured to be the I of my double? What that meant, exactly, wasn't clear, except that I no longer felt afraid. The I of my double was unafraid, that is. Death had been met, the gate at the end of time set ajar, entrance to an afterlife of eternal peace swung open. There was nothing to fear, no one to fear. Whoever I now was would persist, would never perish. I'd been chosen. Still, I did not like feeling so feverish.

I resumed gnawing grooves on my calendar. Day by day I felt better. On bright mornings sunshine sliced through the leafless maples, gilding the pond. Sometimes a chill fog rolled in to curtain off the world. Whether in the warmth of sun or pelt of rain, I took to standing on one leg, head tucked under a wing, pondering. There was nothing else to do. I had no idea if I would ever fly again. I frankly believed I would not—and, like Louis, spend the rest of my days on earth sequestered in thought. But I, the unafraid I of my double, was content to wait—simply, to wait. Was this the state Louis had reached—serenity? How can you really know if someone needs to be rescued? For that matter, how can they know? Perhaps Louis' abduction was in some way for his benefit. What bird can see into the future, to know when it's time to intervene, what to prevent, what to let pass? Was Phoebe's fate ordained?

Isolation was less demanding, I realized, once a drake had been unburdened of his worries, felt assured of his immortality. Before I had died and come back, the mere passage of time stirred in my gizzard a certain lonely apprehension of some conspiratorial threat to my safety, as if in each living moment I'd had to be prepared for a final corporal punishment that would be inflicted in the next instant, which would result it my extinction—a constant, primal undercurrent of fear, a suppressed terror of the imminent. It felt as if this quickening premonition was an ancient legacy, locked away deep in my bones, heavier than my burden of shame and guilt over the murders of Madeline, Father and Phoebe. In this, Louis had been right—his notion of something evil lurking at the end of "time in a straight line."

But of course what might be imminent was a figment my imagination. I could not possibly know what *would* happen next. Yes, every tick of time that drew me forward to the next tick was a yank on an unbreakable harness—that catapulted me into a deceptively familiar yet always somewhat shocking future. It became even clearer to me how what my imagination imagined was nullified every new instant by some unexpected twist. This new instant then became the present instant—the *now*. And from each tick of the *now* gushed a torrent of activity and sensation, more than I could begin to engage with or comprehend—vitality spewing into reality.

This was too much for my brain to deal with, or even the I of my double. I settled into my nest and dozed off.

I awoke with a start. It was dusk. Melody stood before me, shining as pure and white as a full moon. My heart leapt with joy. I shouted her name.

"Not to fuss, dear," she said, the timbre of her voice like distant thunder, "but you were rather difficult to track down."

"Melody! I missed you so much but I couldn't find Louis and the Smorgasbird lured me to Troy's flock and I got some of Belle's brood out and I got sick and died and saw the gate to the afterlife and came back as the I of my double and I'm not afraid of the future!" So much for my serenity.

"Well, dear, I'm sure I'll adore both of you, but I hope you'll fare better than poor Brace. One mind is more than sufficient for anyone, really. And it's quite normal to be afraid. Goodness knows how often I am. A little company now and then helps scads. Oh, and the future, brief as it is, always ends up for the best, love, so we must make it a habit to look on the bright side, mustn't we?"

"Brief? But what about the afterlife?" I cried.

"Ah, the afterlife. Infinite time, infinite love. Abundance always cheapens things, doesn't it, dear." She drew closer. "Except, perhaps, courage. I often think of my father. He knew himself so well."

"But I'm not afraid, now," I said.

"The relief of the recently spared is often temporary," Melody answered. "A good time to make decisions from the heart, dear."

"What about Louis? Have you found him?"

"Always from the heart, love. You've been through a great deal, Marcel. When courage fails, as courage will, it all comes down to gratitude. A thankful heart, dear — dependable wings to carry you above your fears, you know." With that, her image, so solid and white, began to fade and dissipate until I could see the pond dimly through her, and she was gone. And then her voice said from the place where she had stood, "You have been spared, love, so shall you be burdened."

Then, in puffs of light, the figures of all the birds I had known in Bloedel materialized from the deepening night and assembled en masse along the banks of the pond — Mother, Madeline, Belle, Melody, Nick, Troy and Harold, Jasper on his bully pulpit, Cyrus and Alexander, Phoebe and all my kin and friends — all but Father and Louis. Each was swathed in a scintillating aura which somehow fanned out in rainbows of emotion that seemed to exactly express our bonds — affection, trust, suspicion, reverence, contempt, anger, remorse. And from out of those feelings welled up a single conviction — I was at last myself among birds and I was thankful, so very thankful. I could feel my own aura pulse with a distinct energy, the equal of any; whereupon, Father's image also formed before me and the shimmering edges of our auras met and I felt such a surge of indebtedness that my gizzard convulsed and I regurgitated dinner. Then all the auras faded and winked out. I heard the croak of the Smorgasbird and the stiff strokes of his wings as he passed overhead, low and barely visible, dark against dark.

I couldn't depart my pond until I had produced my egg, which, of course, is this story, this confession, my record of inward migration — the offspring, somehow, of my double and myself. A story is catharsis for us ordinary birds, how we can begin to forgive ourselves for our weaknesses and know our true hearts. Perhaps it is the one migration asked of us by the Creator. Before he dies, a drake will be given an opportunity to re-hatch himself, molt in spirit, to birth anew in his own truth and plot. In this way he can indeed decide how to be for the rest of his time, be it an hour or a decade.

I think I am set on the right course. Though I would be saddened to lose the power of flight, to be barred access to the ineffable third earthly dimension — I would not be devastated. I am ready for the Creator to take me — again, at his will, according to his own plan. If he guards access to an even loftier dimension than the sky, of which I believe I had a glimpse, I hope that time there is also limited — may he forgive me for this presumption — so to retain its value.

Epilogue

Soon, my plumage had grown in. Immediately I had launched and gained the tree line, I could see Smorg Lake, it's noxious turquoise sheen, the pocket of sickly ducks — jetsam of my brother's failed command — and the squat gray building on the north shore, from which humans ejected their poisons into the world.

Somewhere in the distance, to the southeast, lay Bloedel — home, Mother, and the family I longed to be with again. My shoulder tendons ached but the exhilaration of restored flight shot through my arteries like sunlight. I flapped up to a low, puffy cloud and played — skimmed its edges, the damp wisps and vapors curling around me. I rolled and looped, veered away, stiffened wings and soared in an updraft like an eagle.

Disused muscles and joints soon fatigued. I set a heading for the lake. The boat had begun its daily crossing and the ducks were swimming out to meet it. I couldn't yet see which of them was Belle. I circled above until the human had dumped her load over the gunwales, then I splashed down in the middle of the feeding flock.

"Marcel!" Belle cried out, her eyes bright.

The ducklings swam beside her. Even disfigured love binds. They had returned — all, that is, but little Marcel. He was my personal Phoenix, I liked to imagine, a perished mallard returned to the world.

A chunk of food was drifting towards me. New decisions had been made. I readied myself.

I carry on Mother's tradition. Each evening, the flock gathers in the cove. As a duck, I speak here to my own kin, but it would bring me contentment should any bird, webfoot or talon, find my account, if not edifying, at least entertaining, that humor at my expense might give pause to would-be liberators, so wasteful of time, who would seek to rescue the world before having first been rescued. Such means are given all birds — wings of truth, acceptance and gratitude.

I doubt if I will ever find Louis — or how I might have the chance to search further. Do I betray him? If it seems so, may he forgive me and know that I have suffered as he, and now in making clear choices I become more trustworthy.

About the author

A fter raising a family and retiring from a career in industry, Donald Berk received an MFA in writing from Bennington College, Vermont, and earned an FAA flight instructor certificate. He now writes and teaches flying in Yakima, Washington. *In Search of Wings Lost* is his first novel.

Made in the USA
Charleston, SC
18 November 2009